*Whinnies on the Wind*
*Volume 7*

## Summer of Desperate Races

by

## Angela Dorsey

www.ponybooks.com

**Original Title:** Summer of Desperate Races
**Cover Design:** 2013 Marina Miller
Printed in the USA, 2013

ISBN: 978-1-927100-28-8

**Enchanted Pony Books**
www.ponybooks.com

# Summer of Desperate Races

## Angela Dorsey

Also at *Enchanted Pony Books*

## Whinnies on the Wind Series

Winter of the Crystal Dances
Spring of the Poacher's Moon
Summer of Wild Hearts
Autumn in Snake Canyon
Winter of Sinking Waters
Spring of Secrets
Summer of Desperate Races
Autumn of Angels
Winter of the Whinnies Brigade

## Sun Series

Sun Catcher
Sun Chaser
Sun Seeker

## Horse Guardian Series

Dark Fire
Desert Song
Condor Mountain
Swift Current
Gold Fever
Slave Child

Rattlesnake Rock
Sobekkare's Revenge
Mystic Tide
Silver Dream
Fighting Chance
Wolf Chasm

## Single Titles

Abandoned

# Chapter 1

Twilight's teeth were clamped together like two sides of an iron vise as we stood together in front of the barn. Still, I optimistically raised the snaffle bit toward her mouth.

"Please, pretty please... Pretty please with sugar on it?"

Okay, I know what you're thinking. Begging is pathetic – but nothing else had worked, and maybe, just maybe, Twilight would be touched by the desperation in my voice.

Or maybe not.

My gorgeous buckskin filly stretched her neck and lifted her head an inch further from my reach, something I'd thought was impossible. The edges of her eye glimmered white as she strained to peer down at me through her long forelock, messy from tossing her head as she'd avoided the bit.

I lowered the bridle, defeated. There was no way I was going to get that snaffle bit into her mouth, not now, and probably not ever. However, just so she was one hundred percent sure that I understood, Twilight asked, *Finished being mean?*

Yes, you heard right. She talked to me, and yes, she's a horse, an almost three year old mustang to be exact. You see, I'm blessed – or cursed – to be able to understand the emotions and feel the sensations of any horse within my "feeling range" of a mile or so.

Feeling horse sensations is lovely most of the time, like when the mustangs are running and the sun's heat

1

is blown off their slick muscles by the wind of their passing. And there's nothing quite like the drowsiness of a well deserved nap after grazing all morning, or anything so bracing as the splash of cold water on the belly when a horse is cooling itself off in one of the nearby lakes dotting our wilderness.

And there's something even more awesome about Twilight and my totally perfect gray gelding, Rusty. They talk to me in *words*. Rusty was the one who developed the language with me. I've been his girl since I was three years old.

This ability to talk to them is both a good thing *and* a not-quite-so-good thing too. It's awesome to be able to tell them how I'm feeling and to hear the cool things they want to tell me. What isn't so great is that, unless I block out all horse impressions, they can tell what I'm thinking *all* the time – and unfortunately, Rusty doesn't keep his opinion to himself when he doesn't agree with something I do or say. Long story short, he expects me to be as perfect as he is.

It's especially hard to keep him happy when I'm trying to sneak some truth out of my mom. That woman has more secrets than a night owl and I've been trying to discover them for as long as I can remember – but I don't even want to think about that right now. It just makes me mad.

*Finished being mean?* Twilight asked again, her head still high.

*Not mean. Just training*, I thought back, trying not to be grumpy. *No more today*, I added so she'd know I was releasing her and not caving to her stubbornness.

Her head came down and her jaw relaxed, and immediately I felt bad. It wasn't fair to Twilight for me to think she was being difficult. I understood how much she hated the feel of the bit in her mouth. That cold hard metal was even worse to her than the feel of a hackamore squeezing her nose.

I put my arms around her neck and gave her a hug, allowing her earthy scent to engulf me. She bent her head around and nuzzled me – her way of letting me know she wasn't mad at me, that all was forgiven. But with worry jangling like a raw nerve in the front of my brain, I couldn't honestly tell her I was okay too.

What else could I try? I had to get Twilight to accept some form of control on her head, but how? I'd tried everything I could think of and she'd hated every single idea with a passion. Somehow, I had to find something she would bear, and soon; Twilight was getting older and she had to get used to being ridden. Even though Mom had more money than normal right now, she still wouldn't keep feeding a horse that didn't do any practical work for us. And how could anyone ride a horse with no bridle?

I knew Twilight's answer to my question. She wanted me to use thoughts to tell her where I needed to go and then she'd get there however she wanted. Seems to make sense, doesn't it? Except that then *everyone* would be suspicious of my gift/curse. You see, no one but Charlie, the Wild Horse Ranger, and Kestrel, my best friend, know I can communicate with horses – and because I don't want to be considered a freak and dragged away to participate in scientific experiments, I want to keep it that way.

I sighed. *Sorry for being nippy*, I thought, momentarily forgetting that Twilight doesn't like apologies. *Sorry*, I repeated, apologizing for my apology.

3

Twilight laid her ears back and snorted, then sauntered off to graze. I watched her for a few minutes. How could I get her to understand the urgency of the situation?

Wild yipping greeted me from behind the spare stall door as I entered the barn. Rusty and Twilight still shared a stall, and the second stall was Cocoa's, Mom's dark brown horse. We used to only use the spare stall for Twitchy, Kestrel's horse, when Kestrel came to visit, but right now it held Rascal, my new and very exuberant puppy. I hadn't wanted him bumbling about, ruining my training session with Twilight. Instead, Twilight got to do that all by herself.

I opened the door and my patchy, multi-coloured pup scooted out, his eyes – one blue and one brown – searching, his nose twitching, his ears perking this way and that. He ranged around, sniffing and snuffling, then followed me to the tack room, where he quickly snapped the mousetrap in the corner, then yelped and rushed out of the room, the mousetrap probably already forgotten. No doubt he was hoping to find Socrates or Plato, our barn cats. He loved chasing them and hadn't many opportunities lately because they'd gotten wise to him. These days they peered down smugly from the loft above and meowed temptingly – the cat version of fun.

I followed him out of the tack room just in time to see him head after Twilight.

"Rascal!" I called, and just like every other time I'd called him, he kept running. We were still working on the concept of coming when called.

*Please be nice to him!* I quickly communicated to Twilight. My instant panic might seem a little extreme, but remember, I *feel* how irritating she finds him. If he got too close to her, she just might kick his teeth in.

She didn't bother responding and when Rascal went for her hind legs – he had strong herding instincts being a border collie – she lashed out. However, I could see the compassion in her kick. She missed him by an inch; Twilight never misses unless she wants to.

Rascal yelped again and ran toward me, his protector, but halfway back, he stopped and quirked his ears toward the cabin. A split second later, he was off, his little legs a blur.

"Rascal!" I called again, though I knew I was wasting my breath. I hustled the rest of the way out of the barn to see what had interested him so much.

Kestrel was riding up to our cabin. Yay!

I hurried toward her. She came once a week in the summer for an overnight visit and lately her visits were the high points of my life. Mom wasn't much of a conversationalist at the best of times, but these days she was even more hermit-like than ever. Though talking to Rusty and Twilight keeps me sane, it's always nice to have another person to talk to.

Mom came out on the porch and Kestrel pulled Twitchy to a halt, then bent down and handed something to Mom; I couldn't see what because Twitchy was in the way. Then Kestrel rode toward me.

"Hey!" she called and waved.

I waved back. "Hey!"

Behind her, Mom strode away from the cabin, her arms swinging and something white fluttering in her hand – an envelope. Before I could even yell, she ducked into the forest and disappeared beneath the shadowy canopy.

Rascal ran after her, and even though I knew Mom wouldn't appreciate his company, I didn't bother trying to call him back. It was good he was going. I'd seen her on her walks lately. She'd storm along with a scowl on her face, like she'd just gotten in a fight with someone and was replaying the entire argument through her mind again and again and again. She'd hardly noticed anything going on around her. The reason I knew? Last week she'd stomped right toward me, arms swinging, and her mind obviously elsewhere. I had to jump aside or I swear she would've trampled me.

This side of Mom was totally new, emerging right after we got back from Vancouver last spring. While there, she'd sold some of her paintings, which you'd think was a good thing; it was how we bought food and clothes and other important stuff. But then she'd changed into this obsessed, striding creature. She hadn't even started a new painting since she got home. The only thing she seemed to do other than walk was write and mail letters, without letting me glimpse the recipient's name, of course. She'd even gotten a couple replies but she kept them a secret too. Maybe I should—

*Dishonest*, thought Rusty, instantly reading my idea to snoop through her stuff while she was gone. I had no choice but to reassure him that I'd never do such a thing. And I wouldn't, mainly because I actually wanted to ride Rusty again. If I upset him, he might make that difficult. And besides, I don't like disappointing Rusty; he's also my hero.

*Sorry*, I said.

I felt Rusty settle happily under his tree behind the barn, then flip at a fly with his tail. He adored summer.

6

*We follow too.*

Twilight was trotting toward me. She'd sensed my worry about Mom.

*Not today.* I knew I couldn't learn anything by following her, yet again. Heaven knows I'd done it enough times already. And besides, Kestrel was here.

"So… doing the horse telepathy thing again?"

I looked up. Kestrel was leaning on her saddle horn as Twitchy stood, one hind leg at rest and ears flopping to the sides, looking like she'd been standing there for hours. Kestrel stretched and yawned, just to rub it in.

"Sorry," I said. I sure seemed to be apologizing a lot lately.

"So what's up?"

"I think Twilight's going to follow Mom." Twilight loped toward the spot in the forest where Mom had disappeared. "What did you give her?"

"Another envelope. Still no return address," Kestrel said, guessing my next question.

"But still the Vancouver postmark?"

"Yeah."

Who was writing to my mom? Where did the letters go that she gave to Kestrel to send? You'd think that last question would be easier to answer, but the envelopes were always addressed to a post office box in Vancouver. No name. No street address. It was beyond frustrating, especially since I was dying for some answers to the questions I'd had since I was old enough to question at all. Why was my mom a hermit? Who were we hiding from, living out here in the wilderness?

I'd gotten a few answers – or should I say a few more *questions* – last spring when I stowed away in the back of Mom's truck during her Vancouver trip. I'd spent an entire day investigating her mysteries and discovered something that shocked me. The people who had been searching for her for years were *family*. I saw a girl, a few years younger than me, who looked suspiciously like me. And there was her grandmother – our grandmother, I suppose – who looked so severe that I wouldn't be surprised if she was the one Mom was hiding from. And then the truly scary thought: I deduced that the only reason Mom had been hiding for all these years from family was because she was hiding me from them. Why? What was she scared of? Was there something weird about them? Would they hurt us if they found us?

See what I mean about more questions?

"Let's turn Twitchy out and get busy." I was so beyond tired of obsessing over this.

"What are we doing today?" Kestrel asked, dismounting.

"It's a surprise."

It didn't take long to get Twitchy untacked and into the pasture. She's always quick and eager when it comes to finishing her day. Her anticipation was delightful to feel. Hanging out with Rusty and Cocoa? There was nothing better in her mind. She almost made me want to go relax with them all afternoon too, but I refrained. Kestrel probably wouldn't find it as much fun.

Loonie, our gray muzzled German Shepherd, rose from her bed by the front door as we walked toward the cabin. She's fourteen years old, just like me, but for a dog, especially a big dog, that's *old*. She stretched and limped toward us, totally unaware of what was to come. When she neared us, she flopped to the ground, tired from her excursion.

"Good girl, Loonie," I murmured and bent to scratch her head.

"So what are we going to do?" Kestrel asked again.

Loonie tipped her head so I could rub behind her ear.

"We're going to give Loonie a bath."

"Great," Kestrel said, sounding as sarcastic as only she and Twilight can sound.

"Come on, she'll love it. Being all pretty again? She doesn't feel pretty very often anymore. And besides, she's filthy."

"Yeah, on the filthy thing anyway," Kestrel said, sounding resigned this time.

First, we heated the bathwater on the wood stove, then dragged the washtub out onto the porch.

"Are you sure your mom won't mind? I mean, this is the tub that you guys bathe in, isn't it?"

"She's not here to ask," I said innocently.

"But what if it gets all gross?"

"I'll rinse it good before she gets home. She won't even notice."

Now where was Loonie? Ah, there she was, cowering against the log walls and watching me with glazed-over, white-rimmed eyes. She was going to love this so much. The warm water soothing over her skin, the beautifully scented soap – surely Mom wouldn't mind if I used her soap – and then the towel rub afterward.

I dumped some cold water into the tub, then hurried inside to get the hot water off the stove. They should make a nice temperature once mixed together. Very carefully, I lugged the steaming pot of water outside and dumped it into the tub, then felt it with my hand. Perfect!

Now where was Loonie? Not leaning against the log wall anymore, nor was she in her usual bed by the door. I skipped down the porch steps. She wasn't under the porch. I looked over the fence into the garden, to see only tall, healthy plants waving their leaves at me in the warm breeze. Behind the cabin, there was just the view of the blue, blue lake that was our water supply. We didn't have modern conveniences like electricity and running water or even an inside bathroom – which you've probably guessed because otherwise I wouldn't be bathing a dog in a big washtub on the porch.

"Loonie!" I turned a full circle to see nothing but the breeze kick up a riffle across the lake. Flies droned and leaves whispered as they brushed against each other. Lovely. I'd never appreciated the sounds of the wilderness as much as before I went to the city and heard all that *noise*. People who live there must have iron ears.

A bird flapped its wings above me and I looked up to see two sleek cedar waxwings fly overhead. And a horse was approaching. I could hear its soft tread on the forest floor. It had to be Twilight. She must have gotten bored of following Mom.

I headed back around the cabin, leaving Twilight to arrive in her own good time – just in time to see Kestrel leading Loonie from the barn.

"You think she knows she's getting a bath?" Kestrel laughed. "I found her crammed in the corner of the barn, trying to look small."

"Poor Loonie," I said, hugging her. "This will be a fun bath with nice warm water. You'll see." In years past, when she'd needed a bath, I'd usually just coaxed her into the lake and done a bit of swimming with her. And don't ask me how she knew she was the one going into the tub this time when she'd never been bathed there before.

Loonie didn't exactly fight us but she was extremely uncooperative as we got her into the tub. Her muscles were rigid, her legs like boards, as we moved them one by one into the warm water. When we finally got all four legs inside, she stood with her ears sideways, looking like she wished she was anywhere else. Kestrel held her collar, and I grabbed Mom's soap and started to scrub.

Twilight arrived just in time to watch us cupping the warm water over Loonie's body to remove the suds. I swear I heard a horsey mind-giggle when she noticed the expression on Loonie's face.

By the time we were finished, the old girl *almost* looked like she didn't totally hate what we were doing. Still, it was a lot easier getting her out of the tub than it was getting her in.

We towelled her vigorously, hoping that it would deter shaking, but we weren't so lucky. We hadn't made it quite clear of her when she started. Twilight backed up, tossing her head in the fine spray; Kestrel and I shrieked. When Loonie went back to her bed by the door, Kestrel and I used the other towel to dry ourselves and then Twilight.

Still soaked, with a thin skim of dog hair completely coating me, I dragged Loonie out of her bed and set to work with my comb while Kestrel used Mom's brush. Now this Loonie *loved.* She stretched and groaned and smiled in her own doggy way, as I pulled the comb as gently as possible through her lightly conditioned fur – I'd figured Mom wouldn't mind if we used a little of her conditioner too, especially since she wasn't going to know the difference. Everything was going to be spic and span by the time she got home.

The comb raked out wads of hair. I had no idea Loonie had so much loose hair left after shedding in the spring. Soon big clumps were piled around her, and still, we kept combing, kept pulling out loose hair. The piles grew bigger. Bigger. How much hair could one dog hold? We could almost stuff a pillow!

A whirlwind of white, black, brown, and gray suddenly leapt onto the porch. Loonie's excess hair went flying. I opened my mouth to tell Rascal to calm down, and it was instantly stuffed with dog hair.

*Mom*, said Twilight. She'd been dozing beside the cabin as we groomed Loonie, but now she was wide awake – and extremely nervous.

I was too, because Twilight was right. Mom was back. In fact, she was staring at us from the bottom of the porch steps. I looked around at our mess and for the first time, saw it for the disaster it really was. Mucky, hair-clumped water floated in our bathtub. Soggy towels were strewn across the rough boards. Mom's fancy soap was in plain sight, as was her bottle of hair conditioner, tipped and dripping onto the porch now, thanks to Rascal. Hair was sticking to everything, including me and Kestrel, and now Rascal too. In fact, Loonie was the only one who looked half decent.

Mom took in everything, her mouth slightly open as if she didn't know what to say. Then her eyes rested on Loonie. "She looks great," she said, then climbed the stairs, picked her way through the disaster zone, and walked into the house. The door shut behind her.

I blinked a few times. "Did *Mom* just go in the house?" I asked, still not quite believing it. "Or was that an alien?"

Kestrel looked as stunned as I felt. "I think it was your mom."

Rascal, thirsty from his walk, leaned over the edge of the washtub to get a drink, his little tail whipping back and forth. He glanced back at me with his blue eye to reassure me that he hadn't forgotten we needed some more jumping on, and he was just getting a drink first.

I saw a shimmer of gold and black out of the corner of my eye; an elegant horse head darted toward him.

"No!" I yelled.

But I was too late. Twilight hooked her nose under the puppy bum and gave it a flip. Rascal disappeared inside the tub with a sploosh. He came up sputtering, then leapt out of the tub and continued his necessary greeting.

Kestrel screamed and ran, and like the good friend I am, I tried to save her by grabbing Rascal – but he was slippery. He popped out of my grip, then raced ran down the stairs after her.

He got as far as Twilight. A huge grin crossed my face as he stopped and shook. Dirty, muddy flecks flew. Twilight jumped back, but, ha! Too slow!

With little brown spots dotting one side, Twilight trotted away from us in an amazingly fluid high-step, Rascal right behind her, running and shaking. Kestrel and I were long forgotten; after all, Twilight was much more exciting.

I would have called him, or I would have at least *tried* to call him– but I couldn't do anything but gasp and laugh. Kestrel was even worse than me. She was laughing so hard she could only stagger as she made her way back to the porch. She collapsed beside me on a big lump of wet, soggy hair and I couldn't help but laugh harder.

But beneath all the hilarity over the show Rascal and Twilight were putting on for us as they dashed this way and that in the meadow, I felt only terrible worry. Mom had seen the conditioner, the washtub, her special perfumed soap – and had walked into the house without a word of reprimand.

I couldn't hide from the severity of the situation any longer. Yes, I'd noticed she'd changed after our trip to Vancouver and I'd tried to find out why, but it was more out of frustration over her continuing secrets than anything else. Plus I was used to her acting eccentric. However, now I knew beyond any doubt that this was more than Mom just acting weird yet again. Something was seriously wrong. Something had happened in Vancouver that had shaken her to her core.

It was time to move my investigation into high gear – and maybe while I was thinking up brilliant ideas and solving the most persistent mystery of my life, I'd find the solution to Twilight's disgust for bridles too. Now wouldn't that be lovely.

# *Chapter 2*

But a couple of weeks later, nothing had changed with Mom or Twilight. I still hadn't gotten my filly to accept anything other than a halter on her head, nor had I learned a single new thing about what was happening with Mom. Of course, that was partly because I'd been good and followed Rusty's rules. I hadn't snuck into her room to snoop even once, though it would've been incredibly easy. Mom had only become worse when it came to long walks and zoning out. She wasn't even acting like a mom anymore, more like a roommate who totally had her own life going on and only noticed me when I was standing right in front of her. Sometimes not even then.

During the last few months, I'd learned to see her attempts to paint as a barometer of how she was doing. Some mornings she'd get all her paints out and stare at the blank canvas for an hour, fiddling with her brushes, sometimes even mixing colours – and then put everything away – but the last two weeks, she hadn't even glanced at the canvases leaning forlornly against the wall in the corner.

Being an optimist, I tried to look on the bright side but there was only one thing I could find to be very grateful for: we didn't have to worry about money. Mom had made a lot from the sales of her paintings last spring and we'd hardly spent anything at all. That meant we could live for a couple of years without her creating more paintings if we were careful about what we bought.

And maybe she was just taking a holiday… yeah, *right*. Being an optimist didn't mean I had to lie to myself.

Then Kestrel brought two things to our house that gave me a giant leap forward in discovering Mom's mystery: a big brown envelope for Mom and some books for me. Mom closeted herself in her room with her envelope as Kestrel was still pulling the bag of books from her backpack.

"So awesome!" I said, distracted from Mom's envelope by a book cover with a big black horse standing in front of a burning barn.

"I'm going to borrow that one from you first," said Kestrel. "And look at this one too."

"You have to wait until I read it," I said, taking the next book she offered – one with a breathtaking cover showing two magnificent horses standing in a field awash in evening light.

Kestrel smiled. "No way. You're going to be reading that book, or this one here." She flashed another book cover my way – a white Pegasus with silver wings.

"No way!" I snatched the Pegasus book from her. "I've been wanting to read this one since forever."

Kestrel laughed. "I know. So see? You won't mind if I read the other one first." She grabbed the fiery horse book.

"Okay, okay," I conceded with a smile.

Mom's door opened and she leaned out. "What on earth are you girls yelling about?"

"Kestrel got me some awesome books, Mom," I said loudly. It was impossible to keep my enthusiasm out of my voice. "Can I get the money to pay her back?"

Mom's face was expressionless as she stared at me, so I asked her again, thinking she hadn't heard me.

"Sure," she finally said, tight lipped. "Let me get it for you." She disappeared inside her bedroom. "Come in here, Evy."

I shrugged to Kestrel before I followed Mom into her bedroom.

Mom shut the door behind me. Okay, even weirder.

Mom moved toward her dresser. "How much do you need?"

"Thirty dollars."

And then I saw it. The brown envelope she'd received was lying on the bed, ripped almost in half, as if Mom had been too impatient to read the contents to open it neatly. Papers lay in two messy piles, the ones she must've already looked at, faced down, and on top of the other pile – I edged nearer – a photocopy of a birth certificate? Not mine. It was for someone named Tristan...

Mom snatched up the papers and clutched them to her chest. I looked up at her as casually as I could, considering my heart was racing and literally thundering in my ears. A clue! Finally, a real clue!

Mom shoved the papers beneath the ripped envelope, then turned her back on me to pull a zippered pouch from her top drawer. She pulled a twenty and a ten from it.

"Don't ask Kestrel to get you anything more, okay?" she asked, as she handed me the money.

"Sure," I said, still blown away by the clue I'd seen. Who was Tristan? If only I'd had time to read his last name too. Or see his birthdate. That could have told me a lot more.

I moved to the door in a fog. Grabbed the door handle. And then her most recent words struck me. I turned back. "Why not? I thought we were doing okay."

"We are. It's just that... well, we don't want to spend it frivolously."

"But books aren't frivol—"

Mom scowled. She actually *scowled*. At me. I thought I was the one who did the scowling in our relationship. How had things gotten so turned around? *Everything* was wrong these days.

And we were running out of money? That was the only reason Mom would tell me not to buy any more books. She'd never been tight on book money before, when we could afford it.

Mom just stared at me, completely ignoring my question, so I left the room, my thoughts still in a whirl. Where had all our money gone to? We'd had lots just two months ago, and it wasn't like there were any stores around to buy anything. We lived in the bush. And if she'd ordered anything in the mail, I certainly hadn't seen it. There'd only been the books, some super yummy food that we bought in Williams Lake on our drive back home, and the new canvases that she didn't seem interested in turning into paintings.

When Kestrel raised her eyebrows at me, I realized I must look about as intelligent as a zombie, standing outside Mom's door with my hand clutching her doorknob. I collected myself as I walked toward her.

"Let's go out to the barn," I said, handing the money to Kestrel and picking up the books. I didn't want to talk where Mom might overhear us.

Kestrel followed me without a word. It didn't take long to explain everything to her. She had no idea who Tristan was either, of course, and what could she say about us being out of money? Whatever Mom had spent it on, Kestrel didn't know about it.

And besides, the answer was obvious. The only way that money could have left our house was in those mysterious envelopes Mom had sent – and if one of the replies contained a photocopy of a birth certificate… maybe Mom's letters were to a private investigator? But who was she having investigated? As always, my clues created far more questions than answers.

Soon I noticed Kestrel glancing sideways at the books, so I took pity on her and stopped ranting. We nestled into the hay in the loft to read my new books – the last new books I'd probably have for a long time – while Socrates and Plato snuggled in beside us, purring. Or to be perfectly honest, Kestrel read and I *tried* to read. Even flying horses couldn't make me concentrate. All I kept seeing in my mind's eye was that birth certificate. When it finally came time to give the horses supper, I was relieved; pretending to read is exhausting work.

Afterward, Kestrel and I fixed ourselves an early supper. We had plans for that night. Mom showed up at the table just long enough to gulp down some food, and then disappeared into her room again – and we were free.

I left a note on the table, just in case she noticed we were gone, telling her we were sleeping out in the barn, which honestly, we were planning to do. Later. Then we grabbed our sleeping bags and pillows, plus a lantern because it would be after dark when we got home. Way after dark, if we were lucky.

As we walked toward the barn, I inhaled deeply and looked up at the glorious sky. We were going to have a fantastic midnight ride. The moon was supposed to be full. The clear sky should show every star. It was the perfect night to look for mustangs. It had been ages since we'd seen Twilight's band, but I'd heard whispers of their presence just yesterday so they were probably still in our area. I was excited to see Twilight's new little sister too, born last spring.

Twilight cavorted around us as we walked out to the barn, she was so excited. Rusty was eager to get out and stretch his legs too. The only one who didn't seem thrilled about our mustang hunt was Twitchy, Kestrel's mare. She's kind of old and doesn't have the energy she used to have. When I suggested that Kestrel take Cocoa, Mom's mare – she hadn't been out for over a week as Mom preferred walking to riding – Kestrel was more than happy to agree.

Rascal howled after we locked him in the spare stall and though I felt bad for him, I knew we couldn't bring him if we wanted to see any wild horses. He hadn't learned to be quiet on command yet, and just one yip from him and the mustangs would be gone. Plus, I knew he wouldn't howl for long. He usually fell asleep within five minutes of being locked up, so I only needed to feel guilty for a few minutes.

Twitchy didn't even wish to come with us as Kestrel and I loped our horses across the meadow and dove into the forest.

The sinking sun streaked a ruddy glow through the branches, covering us with rosy dapples. Rusty's were a rose gray, Cocoa's a dark velvet red. Twilight glimmered with flashy golden pink patches, though her mane and tail remained as dark as night as she danced around us, her nostrils flaring. Kestrel and I rode silently for a while because it was just so beautiful it seemed a crime to speak.

But when the sun dipped behind the mountain, and the long evening began, we couldn't keep our tongues still. There was just so much to talk about. The rodeo was the next weekend, and once again, we were entering in the gymkhana events. I even had a crown to defend. Last year, Rusty and I had won the barrel racing by a fraction of a second. We had to do even better this year because now there was an additional reason to win – it sounded like we could really use the one hundred dollar first prize. Hopefully, this year I wouldn't have to save any horses from their cruel owners, and could give the money to Mom.

Kestrel was entering Twitchy in every race this year too, but she didn't have much of a chance of winning the barrel race. Twitchy wasn't nearly fast enough. However, I'm sure that horse could pole bend in her sleep. Also, the keyhole race was a good one for Twitchy. She was *really* good at stopping.

And then there was the fact I was going to see Jon at the rodeo, or I hoped I would anyway. It's not like I could phone him and ask him if he was going to be there since I didn't have a phone – and had, in fact, only used a phone once in my life. I know, it's bizarre.

I quickly steered our conversation away from Jon though. I mean, he might even have a real girlfriend now, and if he did, I had to be prepared to not become a weeping pile of goo. Okay, so *exaggeration*. But it would be nice if I could at least act like I didn't care one whit if he did like someone else.

"So what are you guys going to do?" asked Kestrel. "About money, I mean, if your mom doesn't start painting."

I scowled. "I don't know. And that's the worst thing. She's not even trying. Her paints have probably all dried up and she doesn't even know it."

"I wish we could find out what's bugging her. Then maybe she wouldn't be so..." Kestrel's voice faded away.

"So what?" I said, feeling even grumpier.

"Nothing."

"No, tell me." Okay, so I admit it, I was looking for a fight. I know it makes no sense but getting mad at my innocent and caring friend seemed a good way to get out the anger I felt toward Mom.

"No, you're too mad," said Kestrel in her usual honest way.

*Why mad?* asked Rusty.

*Let's run*, said Twilight. Her answer to everything stressful. It seems like a good strategy until you realize she usually runs straight toward trouble, and not away from it.

I sighed, defeated. "Sorry. I'm not mad at you."

"I know."

"I don't know what I can do. About money, I mean. Any ideas?"

"You could get a job on our ranch. Maybe Dad will hire you to do something with the cows if you don't charge much."

"Hey, that's a great idea." And it would have the added bonus of being around Kestrel's family, who are all fairly normal people. I *love* normal people. You can more-or-less count on them to not go all weird on you.

Kestrel shrugged. "You'll have to get permission from your mom though. There's no way he'll hire you unless he knows she approves."

"She won't," I said. "Because then I'd be gone and she wouldn't have me around to completely ignore."

Kestrel cast a sympathetic glance my way.

*Moon*, said Twilight, and through her eyes, I saw a silver sliver appear on the mountain's silhouette. I looked for it myself. There it was, even more vibrant and glorious through my own eyes. "Look," I said to Kestrel and drew in a deep breath of night air. This was exactly what I needed, the freedom of the wilds. No more Mom talk. No more even thinking of her. This was my night out with my friends, and I was going to have fun.

The moon become larger and larger as it rose above the mountains, and then finally a perfect sphere, it lifted into the sky. The night was alive with sounds around us, but even though the moon was bright, we didn't see any living creatures other than ourselves. They were watching us though, creating a loud entourage of croakings, flappings, and twitterings as we moved through the bush.

*A tickle on my long neck as the warm night wind flutters my mane. A feather's touch on my hocks from the slow waving of my tail.*

I stopped Rusty short. The mustangs were near – and this mustang felt familiar. I knew her. Wind Dancer?

"You hear them?"

I nodded to Kestrel.

*My foal breathes evenly beside me as she sleeps, deep relaxed breaths. How I love the serenity of this little one as she rests, her vivacity when she wakes. Such a bright little being.*

I smiled. "They're not too far." I reined Rusty in the right direction. "I can hear Wind Dancer and her new baby."

"The rest of the herd isn't there?"

I asked Rusty to walk super steadily and then zoned into the mustangs again. Night Hawk, the herd sire, was nearby, asleep and dreaming. Black Wing, the new lead mare, was only dozing. I could feel her ears swivelling, listening, to the night sounds. She was a good lead mare, smart and wily. It was going to be hard sneaking up on her.

"We should leave Cocoa and Rusty here, and go the rest of the way on foot," I suggested, thinking of their hooves rustling the twigs and bushes as they walked.

"What about Twilight?"

"You think we can keep her here if we tried?"

Kestrel laughed softly. "Good point."

I turned in my saddle and peered into the shadows. No moving gold caught the silver light. "We're too late anyway. She's already gone."

Rusty and Cocoa settled in to wait as we tied Cocoa to a low branch. There was no need to tie Rusty. He knew we wanted to sneak up on the mustangs. I hugged him around his silver dappled neck, and Kestrel and I headed into the woods.

We were probably quieter than the horses as we tried to walk soundlessly in the direction of the mustangs, but not much. It was hard because the moon's light only penetrated the forest's canopy here and there. Every time we came to some moonlight strewn across the pine needles, herbs, and tree litter, we walked in it for as long as possible. Then, in the shadows once again, we'd feel our way to the next patch of moonlight, usually stepping on all sorts of twigs and crunchy leaves in the process. To mask our approach, I asked Twilight to wait to join her old herd. If the mustangs were thinking about her instead of noticing our bumbling noises, we had a much better chance of getting close to them.

The horses were resting on the other side of a meadow. Because Wind Dancer is a glossy palomino and the lightest coloured in her herd, she glowed bright in the magical light. A few yards away from her, the blue roan colt, Ice – now a stocky, two year old – was the next most noticeable. Night Hawk and Black Wing were both dark, so they totally blended into the night, and Wind Dancer's foal was invisible as well. Charlie, the Wild Horse Ranger, had told me last spring that she was a bay, and now I was guessing a dark bay or I would've seen some slight shape in the vivid moonlight.

Sadness touched me when I suddenly realized that was all of them now. Dark Moon, Black Wing's last foal, had gone out on his own last spring, and the amazing Snow Crystal, that grand old mare, hadn't survived last winter. Two years ago, Willow had been stolen by another stallion. So now there were only the three adults and one baby. As for Ice, even he would only be with the herd for a short time. Soon, he'd follow Dark Moon's example and head out on his own.

Why couldn't things remain the same?

Or on second thought, scratch that. Twilight had once belonged to this herd too. I couldn't imagine life without her.

*Ready*, I thought to my intrepid filly. *Distract.*

From the end of the meadow, I heard a Twilight neigh.

Black Wing and Night Hawk pulled from the shadows and high stepped into the meadow toward us, searching for the one who had called to them. Ice right behind them, his head high and the moonlight glimmering off his ridged muscles. He was amazingly elegant for such a stocky young horse. His neck was like a swan's as he pranced after his herd leader and sire. The three stopped where we couldn't see them because of the tree trunks surrounding us.

Twilight neighed again.

"Let's go," I whispered to Kestrel, then tiptoed toward the meadow's edge. The three came into view, standing like statues in the moon's glow, their ears straining toward Twilight as she walked toward them.

Kestrel and I hunkered down behind a big log. It was the perfect place to watch from, because as long as we held super still, our heads peering over the log would look like big broken branch nubs or maybe even fungi.

Wind Dancer approached behind the three luminous statues, followed by a small dark shadow etched around with moonlit brightness. I could feel the foal's heart hammering inside her chest as she reacted to the herd's excitement. Not scared. Thrilled. As she drew near us, a long curved mark on her forehead caught the light – a star in the shape of a scimitar or the new moon.

*Crescent Moon*, I thought to Twilight. *Perfect name for her.*

Twilight didn't respond. She was concentrating on her family, and she knew as well as I did that horses chose their own names.

Wind Dancer stopped beside the other three and watched Twilight walk toward them – but the foal kept going. With her heart thudding a mile a minute, she approached Twilight. What a brave little creature! Wind Dancer began walking again, her gait relaxed. She knew Twilight wouldn't hurt her little sister.

The new foal reached Twilight and the two of them stopped. Sniffed noses. The foal chewed the air and Twilight nickered gently and bobbed her head, then rubbing her little sister's neck.

"Aw," Kestrel whispered beside me.

"Too cute," I gushed quietly.

Suddenly, Night Hawk bellowed and half reared, then rushed forward to greet Twilight. He was a good sire though – careful of the foal, chasing her off before sniffing noses with Twilight. Ice was right behind Night Hawk and the group made a dark huddle in the middle of the meadow. Black Wing seemed to be the only one not overly ecstatic to see Twilight, but that didn't surprise me. They'd never gotten along. Twilight still resented the fact that Black Wing had bossed her around so much when she was young and still lived with the herd – and I can attest to the fact that Twilight *hates* to be bossed.

The group leapt into a run. Ah, this was what I'd been waiting for! They glimmered like silver gilded shadows as they flowed over the ground, around the meadow, kicking, bucking, striking, squealing. It was joyful mayhem as they raced past our hiding spot once, then twice, then three times, sometimes just yards away. And amongst all those big bodies, a little dark shadow flitted here and there – the filly I thought of as Crescent Moon. So brave, so beyond adorable, total cuteness overload.

For the next half hour, Kestrel and I watched the horses play with each other, then they settled down to graze side by side. Crescent Moon stood beside her big sister Twilight, copying her until she was so tired she could hardly stand. When Wind Dancer finally called

27

her, she gratefully went back to her dam, had a quick snack, then sunk to soft summer grass to sleep.

Kestrel yawned beside me, and I totally caught it and yawned too.

*Going home*, I said to Twilight. Though tired, Twilight put on a little rearing show for her buddies, holding their attention as Kestrel and I faded back into the forest. I enjoyed feeling the mustangs' amusement as they watched Twilight cavort around – it felt like feathers tickling my insides.

Rusty and Cocoa were sound asleep when we got back to them. Quickly, we retightened our cinches and climbed aboard. They moved lethargically toward home.

"Is Twilight coming?" Kestrel asked once we were out of earshot of the wild ones.

"She'll probably stay the night. But wasn't that awesome? I haven't seen them that close for a long time."

"It was... indescribable." I could hear the smile in Kestrel's voice as she said the words. "The way they ran around and played under the moon? Some people would die to see that."

"I was scared for Crescent Moon a couple of times though. She's so little."

"Aw, what a cute name."

"Well, she hasn't chosen a name yet. I just picked that one."

"It's perfect for her. And I know what you mean about being worried about her. There were a couple of times I almost yelled to warn her. It reminded me of—" Kestrel gasped.

"What?"

"That's it! The way for you to make some money. Some *real* money."

"What? Tell me."

"Don't you see? The rodeo? Horses running around like crazy? All jumping and leaping and racing, just like in the—"

"Downhill Mountain Race!"

"Yes!"

Kestrel was a genius. It was the perfect suggestion. A little risky, maybe, but… Rusty swished his tail. Okay, so there was no maybe about it. The race was risky. In fact, some might call it dangerous. Others, even highly dangerous. There's something about racing down steep hills dotted with trees, boulders, and drop offs, peeling out around tight corners in the few sections with trails, and plunging across fast flowing rivers, all within three quarters of a mile, that some people consider unsafe .

Or maybe it's the speed they don't like. After taking twenty minutes to climb the small mountain, it takes the contestants and their horses about a minute and a half to get to the bottom.

But I didn't care if it was dangerous. It was still the perfect solution. First, I knew there was a nice prize. Second, I was allowed to go to the rodeo. Third, Mom wouldn't be there to stop me. Fourth, and most important of all, if I won, I'd be doing my bit to help solve our problems with money, which made me feel good about myself.

And I knew because I was trying hard to do the right thing and not being even a little bit selfish by thinking of spending the money myself, that I'd do well. I mean, the forces of goodness would be behind me. Right? Right!

# Chapter 3

The morning of the rodeo dawned dark and dreary. The sky looked like it had been stuffed with massive billows of cotton and then had ink poured over them. Great. Two major races to run, both extremely important to win, and it was pouring, making every single racetrack within miles all sloppy, slippery, and slimy. Not fair, especially since just a few hours ago, the sky had been studded with stars and the full moon had smiled down like a big friendly grandma face in the sky.

I slid from under my covers and padded into the main room of our cabin. Mom wasn't up yet, but that was normal – or it had been normal for the last few months. Wistfully, I thought back to when she used to make me pancakes in the mornings on special days, before she turned all weird. I missed those old days. And not just because of the food. The best part of the breakfast ritual had been spending time with Mom. I missed *her* far more than her to-die-for pancakes.

Her bedroom door flew open so hard that it smacked against the log wall. Mom stood in the doorway, her hair and eyes all wild like she'd just leapt out of bed and was now late for the most important meeting of her life. "Are you ready to go yet?" she asked so fast that it sounded like one long, very loud word.

"Uh..."

Mom strode toward the kitchen area. "I'll make you some breakfast and then you can get on your way."

"Uh..."

"Some granola would be good, right?" She jerked the big bin of bulk granola out of the cupboard and thunked it down on the counter, then snatched the lid off, grabbed a bowl and scooped some out.

"I have to take care of the horses first," I said as she marched to the table, the full bowl in one hand and a jar of milk in the other. I didn't wait for her to answer; I bolted toward the door.

Safe outside, I gave Loonie and Rascal their morning pets and scratches – *quickly*, just in case the crazy granola lady decided to follow me, bowl and milk in hand – and then headed off through the dwindling rain to the barn.

"Come, Rascal," I called even though the pup was already bounding toward me. I figured the best way to teach him to come when called was to call him every time he was planning on following anyway. Loonie would come if I called, but I didn't want her to feel obligated to follow me for nothing. She needed to conserve her energy for her naps.

"Good boy, Rascal," I said as he bounced along behind me, then promptly forgot all about him. Mom had totally freaked me out. What was wrong with her? All of a sudden, she was not only into feeding me, but *fiercely* into feeding me. Had she realized her neglect and now was going overboard to make up for it?

A flash of anger touched my heart. She'd been ignoring me for months. No way was I just going to forget all that and eat her granola, even if I was hungry.

I headed for the tack/feed room as soon as I reached the barn, and scooped out oats for the three horses. Rusty and Twilight got lots because they were coming to the rodeo with me, and Rusty especially needed the energy that oats would give him for his two races.

31

Cocoa was probably just going to hang around home, but I didn't want her to feel depressed about being the only one not getting any goodies, so she got half as much as the others.

The sky was brighter and the rain had turned to bug spit by the time I carried their grain buckets outside and called them. The trio stopped grazing and ran toward me, looking all healthy, sleek, and gorgeous, and I felt my shoulders relax, my breathing become deeper, and my resentment toward my mom fly away.

I lifted the buckets to the other side of the fence, being sure to keep one of them quite a distance from the others, then leaned on the top rail to watch my three friends run the last few yards.

Rusty and Twilight were like two peas in a pod; they never fought, so it didn't matter if their buckets were right beside each other. Cocoa, on the other hand, didn't like anyone near her as she ate. Just like Twitchy, she was a little protective of her oats. In fact, if you put two buckets of oats on each end of a massive field, one for Twitchy and one for Cocoa, they'd still glare at each other across the expanse with their ears back and their tails switching, sure that the other was going to try to steal her oats.

Right now though, Cocoa looked totally relaxed. She not only trusted Rusty to stay away from her oats, but to keep Twilight from snatching mouthfuls too. Grain dribbled to the ground as she chewed her treat and smiled.

A multi-coloured blur dashed under the fence.

"No!" I squawked.

My cry made no impact on Rascal as he made his play for the tiny oat morsels falling to the ground. But he sure noticed Cocoa when she shot after him, teeth bared and front hooves stomping.

Invade the sacred space? Take that! And that!

Rascal screeched to a stop, instantly terrified, then lunged for the fence and safety. Cocoa's yellow chompers were less than an inch behind him as he tumbled under the bottom rail. Once safe, he didn't slow down. His little patchy bottom rocketed away from me as he yipped in terror.

"Rascal!"

He slowed.

"Rascal, come!"

Oh my gosh. Could it be? Or were my eyes playing tricks on me?

No. Rascal was actually stopping after I called him. He was actually listening to me. Actually *obeying*.

"Rascal, come. Rascal, come!"

And my sweet little pup ran back to me! Unbelievable! At long last, he'd understood that when I said 'come' I wanted him to run toward me. Not away. Not toward Twilight or Loony. Not around the back side of the cabin to play in the lake. "Come" actually meant, "Run to Evy" – at long, long last.

And not only was he running toward me, his little ears flapping behind him, but he was running to me while the big scary Cocoa stood just a few feet away. True, she was on the other side of the fence, but still.

I swept him up into my arms and snuggled his squirming, licking self. "Good boy, Rascal! You wonderful, perfect, little cutie-wutie. Did the big mean Cocoa-Wocoa try to bite my little Goofy-Woofy?"

Okay, okay, so I know I'm pathetic. But Rascal loves that kind of mushy talk and he was the one I wanted to both cheer up and reward – he'd finally understood the coming-when-called thing. Amazing! And so suddenly.

Almost weirdly suddenly.

And just as bizarre, the rain chose that moment to stop. Sunlight burst through the clouds in bright streaks.

I gasped. Could today be one of *those* days? Just like when there are days when everything seems to go wrong, there are days when *everything goes right*. And if today was a right kind of day, maybe I could bring out Twilight's bridle this instance and hold the bit up to her mouth and she'd open wide. Maybe I could just ask Mom what was bothering her so much that it was ruining our relationship, and she'd just tell me. Maybe we'd eat pancakes together and laugh and talk like we used to. And maybe, just maybe, Rusty would not only win the Downhill Mountain Race *and* the Barrel Race, but the Stakes Race too.

Okay, so that was too much. No way could Rusty ever beat Twitchy at the running the Stakes. It was a universal impossibility.

And there was no more time for daydreaming. I had to get ready for the rodeo.

Rascal looked at me with his sad blue eye and even sadder brown eye, totally sucking up the sympathy as I baby-talked and carried him back to the house.

I slowed as I drew near our cabin. Had Mom gone back to her room or was she still lurking about with the cereal bowl and milk? Suddenly, running in the Downhill Mountain Race didn't seem like the scariest thing I'd do today.

Maybe I could just wear my pyjamas to the rodeo, and who needed clean teeth? But my money was inside too,

34

and I'd need every cent of it my meagre funds to enter the races today. I was going to have to be brave.

I put Rascal beside Loonie on the porch and smiled when he snuggled up to her, moving in for a little more compassion. What a suck. Then quietly, sooo quietly, I opened the front door of the cabin and leaned inside.

Mom had her back to me at the wood cook stove. Whew! Now, if I could just get to my room without her seeing me. I tiptoed inside and turned back to close the door silently behind me. Rascal and Loonie stared at me though the sliver of open door as it narrowed, narrowed…

A pathetic whimper slid from Rascal's throat.

No!

I spun around just in time to see Mom turn and look at me.

"Thanks, buddy," I whispered out of the side of my mouth.

"I'm sorry, Evy," Mom said, her voice not high or shrill or rushed or anything. In other words, she sounded like my real mother for the first time in months. "I didn't mean to push you this morning," she added.

Not trusting that everything was fine, I hurried toward my room. "I just need to get dressed. Then I'll go."

"But I'm making pancakes."

I stopped, somehow unable to believe my ears. "What?"

"I thought we deserved a treat, so I made pancakes."

A huge smile crawled onto my face, leaving me speechless. While I was at the barn, Mom had hauled wood and lit a fire so she could heat the stove, then she'd mixed up the batter, which was more than just batter. She always put in apple chunks, and if I was lucky, even pieces of dried apricots and cranberries. "Really?"

Mom smiled. "Yes, really. It's been too long."

I grinned back at her, my resentment melting like ice cream in the blazing sun. "Thanks, Mom." We were going to pancake heaven.

Mom turned back to the frying pan on the wood stove, her pancake turner in hand. "Well, I know you're having a busy day."

I almost floated to my room, I was so happy. Mom was acting *normal*. She was speaking to me as if she was actually interested. She was making pancakes. This *was* my lucky day. That Stakes Race was going to be mine, despite Twitchy's gift.

A few minutes later, Mom and I sat across from each other at the table. A massive pancake filled my plate. I cut off one huge bite and shoved it into my mouth. This pancake didn't need syrup; not when pure fruity, cinnamon goodness was baked right inside.

By the time I tore myself away from the table, my belt was straining. Mom gave me a big hug and wished me luck in the barrel race, her face looking open and honest and unclouded with secrets.

"Why don't you come with me, Mom?" I asked without thinking. Immediately, I wanted to bite my tongue. There was no way I could enter the Downhill Mountain Race if she came. But then, doing something fun with Mom would be worth the loss. There would always be more races.

Her open smile slid away and the hood descended, instantly clouding her face again. "I can't. Not today."

I nodded as I fought my disappointment. Of course she wouldn't come. I'd been an idiot to think she might.

"Good luck," she said again, and then quick as a flash, leaned to kiss me on my forehead. Then she was pushing my raincoat at me in case the rain started again and giving me money so I could buy some lunch. The next thing I knew, the door was shutting behind me.

A few minutes later, still kind of stunned, I rode out of the yard on Rusty, with Twilight bouncing around us like a golden, horse-shaped basketball.

Kestrel was eager to get going by the time we got to her house, and I only had time to say hi to her mom before we were heading out her ranch gates at a lope. So much excitement ahead of us, so much fun, so much—

*Escape... run...* The thoughts were like barely whispered voices.

I stopped Rusty and strained to listen with my horse radar. First, I felt Kestrel's parents' horses, dozing in their corral. Another three horses were ahead of us on the road – ones I didn't know, probably on their way to the rodeo with their people. Cocoa was daydreaming about wildflowers.

Wait. Cocoa?

But that was impossible. Kestrel's ranch was miles from my cabin, far past my normal horse-sensing range.

"What's wrong?"

"Nothing."

Now I was hearing voices that weren't there? Cocoa. Faint whispers of panic that were now totally gone. This back and forth thing with Mom was obviously making me crazy too.

"So why'd you stop?" asked Kestrel, being her usual persistent self.

"No reason," I said and asked Rusty to walk on.

Kestrel raised her eyebrows at me.

"So, this is my lucky day," I said to distract her. "Your Stakes Race crown is at risk."

Kestrel laughed, and my stopping for nothing was forgotten. After all, the rodeo was much more fun to talk about, for both of us.

When we got close to town, I told Twilight that it was time to put on her halter and rope, which was part of our deal right at the beginning. Basically, she was allowed to come if she wore the halter and she wasn't allowed to if she didn't. I was glad when she'd committed to wearing the halter. Too bad the bridle thing wasn't as easy to talk her into.

True to her word, Twilight submitted meekly to being haltered. I wrapped the end of the lead rope around Rusty's saddle horn, then told Rusty and Twilight I had to shut out their voices while we were in town. In fact I could already hardly hear them in the emotional din from all the other horses, even though they were right next to me. Then I put up my mental barriers.

This was something I'd learned to do a couple of years before, thanks to Twilight, and it was totally useful in situations where I felt overwhelmed by the number of horses to feel or their strong emotions. Before I learned the technique, I felt every sensation, mood, and emotion of every horse within range – and as a result, turned into a totally zoned-out, social zombie when it came to talking to humans. Unfortunately, most people don't take a blank "duh" as intelligent conversation. But with the blocking of the horses' thoughts and sensations, I could actually act like most of my fellow humans, or at least enough like them that I didn't stand out too much.

Kestrel started greeting some of the people we passed, and I was happy that I knew a few more people this year too. There was Charlie, the Wild Horse Ranger, leaning on his amazing horse Redwing, talking to another guy I knew, Troy. Charlie nodded as we rode by and I waved. Twilight kicked in their direction, even though I know she likes Charlie, and *really* likes Redwing. In fact, that's probably why she did the kick – her way of saying, *Look at me, aren't I cute?*

And then there was Jon, riding toward us on a tall red roan with flaxen mane the exact shade of Jon's hair waving in the breeze. I sighed. Gorgeous.

The horse I mean.

"New horse, Jon?" asked Kestrel as I tried to gather my wits.

"Hey, Kestrel. Evy. Yeah, this is Cleo. Mom wanted to ride Cole today." Cole was Jon's black gelding.

"Cleo. Cole. Same letters," I said like an idiot.

But Jon didn't seem to notice the idiot part. He smiled. "Hey, cool."

"Maybe you can name your next one Celo or Olec?" Kestrel suggested.

Jon leaned on his saddle horn and looked into me with those blue, blue eyes. "You going in the barrel race this year, Evy?" he asked, all casual.

I nodded.

Jon grinned. "Well, you might have a challenge this time. Cleo's pretty fast."

"Bring it on," I said, feeling a little better. Civilized conversation might be difficult for me, but taunting was something I could do quite well.

"And what about the Stakes Race?" asked Kestrel, getting right into it. "Care for a challenge there?"

"You bet," said Jon, not missing a beat.

"Or the Downhill Mountain Race?" I asked.

Jon straightened. "You're joking. Right?"

"Nope."

"But that race is danger—" He stopped, probably because he didn't want to look nervous in front of a couple of girls. Or maybe in front of a girl he liked? I could only hope.

"Yeah, it's exciting," I said, deliberately misunderstanding what he was about to say. "And Rusty's going to be great at it."

Jon nodded. "Well, you better go sign up. I think the race starts in less than an hour."

"Let's get going," said Kestrel.

We reined our horses away. I glanced back to see Jon still watching us. "Hey, you want to come?" I asked, not thinking of how I'd feel if he said no until too late.

"Sure," he said.

*Yes*! This was total proof. This really was my lucky day.

Or that's what I thought until an hour later when Rusty and I stood beside Kestrel and Jon, watching our competitors with something very close to dismay. The horses were all *much* bigger than Rusty, the riders all *much* older than me, and everyone was *much* louder and more aggressive than all of us combined. Horses leaped about with excitement and anticipation. Riders guffawed and taunted each other. It was pure chaos.

"Get to the starting line," a guy yelled, waving a starter pistol in the air.

"Let's go, buddy," I said and urged Rusty forward. "Let's win this thing."

A horse bumped Rusty from behind and I turned in the saddle to glare – and saw a guy laying into his horse with a whip. I didn't need to read the big bay's mind to see he felt both frustration and pain.

"What are you doing to that poor horse?"

The man scowled at me, then reined his horse away, his whip arm moving with a little less ferocity. I didn't know what to do. Obviously, the bay didn't want to run the race and in an attempt to tell his owner so, was refusing to move to the starting line – but his owner just wasn't getting it. Should I say more to the guy, like that there were other, non-whacking ways to persuade horses to obey? But then I was no expert on persuading horses; I couldn't even get Twilight to accept a bridle.

Then I saw Charlie riding Redwing toward the pair, and relief blossomed. Charlie would take care of things.

Rusty and I waited patiently for all the excited men, women, and their horses to line up. The last one to the starting line was the poor bay. He squeezed in between Rusty and a black mare, panting like he'd already run a race or two. His rider looked just as beat.

"What are you doing here, little girl?" the guy snapped at me, not too tired to be rude. "You and your pony lost or something?"

"Nope," I said. "We're just here to win a race."

He laughed, his good humour restored a little.

"On your mark!" The man with the starter pistol aimed it into the air.

I glanced over at Kestrel and Jon on the sidelines. They looked frozen with fear – or maybe my imagination was simply making them look the way I felt. Twilight pranced on the spot beside them. If I could hear her, I'm sure she'd be asking to run alongside me. I wished she could.

I leaned over Rusty's neck. The racetrack spread out before us, a rough swampy meadow with a white flag at the end of it. The flag wasn't the finish line. No way. We were supposed to follow the flags, first across the boggy ground, then through a thick forest and down a steep mountainside, choked with trees and boulders. Then came the trail and the river, and finally, if the rider was still aboard, flat out across level terrain to the rodeo grounds and the finish line.

Oh. My. Gosh. What on earth was I thinking? This race was *dangerous!*

Blam!

Rusty lurched forward. The man on the big bay jerked his left rein and his horse smashed into us. I almost went flying, but my wonderful Rusty felt me lose my balance and slowed. Someone behind us yelled, "Move over!" – and then I got serious. I was in this race because we needed the money. I *had* to win! No way was some bully on horseback going to make me eat beans all winter.

I righted myself on Rusty's back. *Go!*

Somewhere in the din – yes, I'd forgotten to keep my mind closed in my excitement – I heard Rusty's *Yes!* Such enthusiasm in that yes! I closed my mind to the horse voices again as Rusty darted past the black mare, who was running with her tail in the air – so pretty, but not very fast.

Like a silver streak, we swept past a small bay gelding, then a rangy pinto.

Now the big bay's bum was moving in front of us, a powerful machine that was apparently made to churn up chunks of mud. Rusty and I were pelted with sticky globs as we tried to get past him again and again, but every time Rusty moved to one side and started to gain on him, the bay moved over too, no doubt directed by his hilarious owner. I could have mind-yelled at the poor horse but it wasn't his fault his owner was a jerk.

Because I didn't seem to be taking care of the problem, Rusty decided to take matters into his own hooves and run up on the bay's behind. He was about to take a bite of the big brown butt when all the horses in front of us slowed. We were reaching the forest already.

This was our chance!

Rather than go single file or try to jostle past other horses on the narrow trail, I reined Rusty into the trees. He was the best horse I'd ever seen at bush running. I could only hope he'd be good enough to pass some of the horses racing along the trail.

Rusty raced through the trees like a pro, leaping over logs, running between trunks, crashing through bushes like a wild thing. I didn't dare look sideways, even for a fraction of a second, to see what the competition was doing. It took every bit of my skill and concentration just to duck all the branches and move properly for each obstacle so I wouldn't slow down my amazing horse. And then the sky opened in front of us.

Rusty slid onto his haunches and kind of bumped and leapt down the mountain, sliding around boulders and trees, scrambling to keep his hooves beneath him. Down, down, down we went. Down. Down.

And then the trail was beneath Rusty's hooves and only one horse was running in front of us, a powerful chestnut mare with the longest legs I'd ever seen.

Now that he didn't have to dodge boulders, logs, and tree trunks, Rusty was really able to shine. He stretched low to the ground, despite the fact we were still running downhill, and the chestnut's bum got closer and closer.

A wide spot in the trail was coming up. "Now!" I yelled to Rusty.

But he didn't respond. He couldn't see the wide spot around the chestnut's body, and was probably wondering why I was telling him to run faster when he was almost clipping her back hooves as it was. There was really only one thing to do – open my mind to the horse sensations. One single moment, that's all, just so I could tell Rusty about the wide spot in the trail ahead, and—

*Terror leaps upon me like a wild beast. The ground rumbles beneath my hooves, strange sights whip past. People smell is everywhere. Everywhere! Must escape! Must escape!*

With every bit of mental energy I had, I fought the fear, fought the panic, pushed the horse emotions back, back – and then opened my eyes to see the chestnut a fair distance ahead of us, the wide spot in the trail long past. Rusty was glancing back at me as he galloped along, a worried look in his eye.

Who had I just heard?

But who didn't matter. What mattered was that some horses needed my help. Desperately.

Suddenly, the race didn't feel nearly as important. I grasped Rusty's mane with renewed vigour. "Go!"

And he went!

Within seconds, that chestnut bum was right in front of us again, and then water was flying around us as we plunged into the river. The chestnut stumbled on a rock hidden beneath the surface of the water. Sleek as a seal, Rusty was around her and leaping forward. We lurched up the muddy bank and a split second later, were running flat out toward the rodeo grounds. The cheering people came closer, closer – and then we were inside the rodeo arena. The finish line drew swiftly near. The applause and shouts peaked!

We were across the finish line. We had won!

Rusty didn't slow as we swept around in a big circle and headed back toward the gate. The cheering faded a bit. The spectators were probably wondering what on earth I was doing. As we raced out the big gates again, we passed the chestnut mare galloping into the arena, toward the finish line. The surprise on her rider's face was priceless as we rushed past each other. I could just see him wildly asking himself if there was more to the race that he hadn't known about.

Then the cheers and cries of surprise faded in the distance and the only sound was Rusty's hooves hitting the hard ground as he ran and ran and ran in the direction I'd heard the horses' fear. As his hoofbeats thundered on, I clung to his back with all my strength and prayed that I wouldn't be too late, that the horses would be okay until I arrived, and that whatever was wrong, I'd find a way to save them once I got there.

# Chapter 4

As soon as we were far enough away from the rodeo grounds that I wouldn't be overwhelmed by the massive number of horse feelings surrounding me, I slowed Rusty to a lope along the narrow dirt road, and prepared myself to feel the same intensity of horror that had hijacked me earlier.

Yes, there they were. Still frightened, still panicking, still desperate to escape – but not as loud. Despite our mad, desperate race, we were further from them, which explained the impression I'd gotten from them about the world whipping past. They'd been in a vehicle, probably a big truck with its back open to the air. Thank goodness the impression was no longer there; the truck wasn't moving anymore. If we were lucky, we'd catch up before it carried the mustangs even farther away.

*Hear me? Hear me?* Twilight's thoughts billowed into my mind.

*Yes, hear you.*

*Catching up.*

*Will wait.* My filly's thoughts sounded lovely in my head. How I'd missed our connection. I couldn't believe how infinitely relieved I was to know she was following me – and I could tell she felt as relieved as I did.

I sensed Twitchy too, plus a horse I didn't recognize. Cleo? I hadn't turned my horse radar on when I first her, so wouldn't recognize her now. And Cocoa.

Enough with feeling Cocoa's presence all the time. She was at home—

My hand tightened around the reins and Rusty stopped short. Cocoa was not at home, not even close. She was right in front of me, tied to a tree outside a building up ahead, and she appeared to be sleeping. Parked in the driveway beside her, sat a shiny black convertible.

Mom was in town?

Hoofbeats sounded and I turned to see Kestrel and Jon galloping up behind me, Twilight running free before them like a golden beacon, her head high and her glossy mane and tail flying behind her. Kestrel had taken her halter off, probably so she could help them find me. Lightness touched my heart. How glad I was that she was here, that they were all here.

"What on earth are you doing, Evy?" Kestrel yelled as soon as she and Jon were close enough. They clattered to a stop beside me.

"We have to hurry," I replied. "I'll explain on the way." I'd deal with Mom later. Right now, I had to find those horses before the truck took off. As we passed the house with Cocoa tied out front, Kestrel's mouth dropped open. When she looked at me, dumbfounded, I shook my head. Now was not the time to talk about it.

"I heard some horses. I think they need help," I said, as we loped along.

"You heard them way out here?" asked Jon, clearly being much too practical.

"No, they were in a truck. I'm just following them." My mind whirred as I tried to think of a way to explain to Jon. He didn't know about my gift, and I wanted to keep it that way.

"They drove past you?"

"In a way."

"But there's no road along the race course."

"They drove past the rodeo grounds."

"You heard them neighing from the other side of the rodeo grounds as you were finishing the race?"

Okay, so this was proving to be more difficult than I'd even imagined. "I have supersonic hearing," I said. Rusty suddenly crow-hopped, almost unseating me. He could feel I was stretching the truth. *Sorry*, I thought to him.

"And you could hear they were in trouble by the faint neighs?" Jon asked, not letting it go.

"Um..." How could I answer without disappointing Rusty or giving myself away?

"I bet they were mustangs," said Kestrel, coming to my rescue. "Evy knows every mustang in these parts, don't you, Evy? You probably recognized the neighs."

I could have hugged her. Instead, I nodded. "Yeah, they were mustangs, and no one has the right to catch them. Especially when they're probably going to... you know."

"Yeah," said Jon and Kestrel together. We all knew. Sometimes people would take one or two mustangs from the wild and train them, but never a whole truckload. There was only one reason for that. Someone had rounded up a herd or two or three and was taking them to sell for slaughter.

I quickly zoned into the mustangs. Yes, we were getting closer. Another few minutes at this speed and we'd be there. Rusty would be glad for a rest when we stopped. The poor guy had just run a race.

Minutes later we turned a corner and a long fence came into view, bordering the narrow muddy road. Far down the fence sat two tall posts with a beam on top.

Ranch gates. We pulled our horses to a walk and turned them into the trees beside the road. Stealth was required now. We had to check out the situation and make a plan, and quickly too. Who knew how long the truck would be parked there?

"Are you going to halter Twilight?" Kestrel asked, when she and Jon had tied their horses.

"No, we might need her and Rusty's help." I glanced at Jon just in time to see him look puzzled. "They'll come if I call," I explained. Which was true. I didn't have to tell him I called them with my thoughts.

Jon nodded. "So what are we going to do?"

"Sneak close and see what's happening," said Kestrel.

"Then save the mustangs," I added.

"Yeah," said Jon. "But how?"

"We'll figure that out later," I said. Obviously, Jon was kind of lost when it came to this sneaking around stuff. Fortunately, Kestrel and I had a *lot* of experience with it.

I asked Twilight and Rusty to stay behind until we knew the situation, and then Jon, Kestrel, and I crept through the woods. A couple minutes later, we reached the edge of the forest and a pole fence. A cabin sat a few yards on the other side of the fence, blocking the view of the main ranch yard – and what a filthy looking cabin it was. Our cabin at home was probably half the size, but at least we treated it like we loved it. We brushed off the dirt and cobwebs. We washed the windows.

But on second thought, maybe it was a good thing the windows on this poor home were clouded with grime. No one inside would get a clear view of us.

Kestrel nodded to me and together we ducked through the fence, then raced the short distance to the back cabin wall. We pressed our backs against the rough logs and looked at Jon, still in the trees. He raised his hands, palms up, asking us with his actions what on earth were we doing.

I held out a hand, palm out. He looked more baffled. Maybe we should've gone over the signals before we made our wild dash to the cabin. But what else could a palm facing out mean, but to wait? Or stop?

Kestrel and I headed around the corner of the cabin, silent as shadows. We ducked beneath the one grimy side window and crept toward the front of the building. A big truck, parked across the ranch yard in front of a warren of corrals and enclosures, came into view, the back of it holding five or six frightened mustangs. A huge barn loomed behind them, looking even more neglected than the cabin. There was even a hole in the roof.

There was a flurry of movement in the corral behind the truck. More mustangs? It had to be. How long had these people been stealing horses from the wild – and from right under my nose? Obviously Charlie didn't know about it either. It was his job to protect the mustangs and if he knew these guys had been messing with them, he'd be as furious as I was.

The mustangs' agitation rattled around my brain as I tried to collect my thoughts. We needed a plan desperately. I motioned to Kestrel to stay put – no point in both of us risking capture – and slid along the rough logs closer to the front of the cabin. The truck grew closer, the mustangs more visible.

My heart fell. There was a bay, a couple of chestnuts, a black, and a palomino – no, not a bay, a *bay pinto*. Except for the black, the group in the back of the truck looked like Dancing Coyote's herd, and he could have easily acquired a new mare since I last saw him. The bay pinto was Cricket, I was sure of it. Her new daughter, a beautiful buttermilk buckskin pinto, was probably hiding behind her. And that chestnut with the wild eyes, looking like she wanted to either disappear or kill someone, could only be Wildfire.

I'd met them all last summer when Wildfire and Cricket were tame horses, and I rescued Wildfire from an abusive owner, a really nasty man who learned to lividly hate me within an extremely short period of time. Cricket was given to me because she was chronically lame. I'd turned the two mares loose, hoping the palomino mustang stallion would stop trying to steal Cocoa and Twilight, and my plan had worked. Everyone was happy – until these mustang hunters came along and ruined everything.

The front door opened hard, slamming against the outside wall. I pressed back against the side wall as people stomped out of the house.

"Hurry up," a man growled. "I want to be out of here in ten."

"Sure, Dad." The second guy's voice didn't sound like any kid I'd ever heard. He had to be an adult son.

The two of them headed down the stairs and came into view as they strode toward the truck and corrals, the old guy, big and burly, and the younger man, thin, athletic, and nervous looking.

*Wildfire? Are you there?* I thought.

*EVY!*

I felt like a hero. Not only did Wildfire still know my name, but she was completely confident that I was going to rescue her and her family. And yes, just in case you didn't notice, I can talk to Wildfire too. She, Rusty, Twilight, and a colt that sent me on a number of

51

errands last summer are the only ones I can use the thought-language with, just so you know.

*Mean man*, she added.

*Will you help?* I asked. We didn't have time to discuss the men, and besides, I already knew they were mean. They wouldn't be in the business of catching mustangs for slaughter if they were nice.

*Mean man*, Wildfire repeated, exasperated.

*Yes*, I said back, just as exasperated. *Will you help?*

Her agreement sounded in my head as her relief washed over me again. She thought I had a plan already.

The truck started with a roar, then backed toward the loading chute attached to the corral holding the rest of the mustangs. Fear spiked through every single one of the wild horses, then like an immediate echo, through me.

I leaned forward, intent on seeing everything, despite my racing heart. Whatever happened next would affect our plan. These guys were either going to run Wildfire's herd into the corral – which would mean we had some time to rescue the mustangs – or they'd chase the other horses up the chute and into the back of the truck, which meant they were planning on leaving momentarily with a full load of victims and we had no time at all.

I caught movement out of the corner of my eye and slowly turned my head. A massive dog walked down the porch steps just yards away from me. Thank goodness it hadn't smelled or heard me. How stupid of me to not think there might be a dog. And this fellow was huge, thick and muscular. Kind of like a black lab crossed with a grizzly bear. In other words, big. Very big.

When the dog was halfway to the truck, I jerked my gaze back to the mustangs.

The two men were in the corral, pushing the mustangs toward the chute leading to the truck.

Oh no! My good luck – and the horses' – had just come to a crashing end. There was no time to lose.

I sprinted back to Kestrel and Jon, now both standing near the back wall of the cabin. "They're loading the rest of the mustangs right now," I said in a loud whisper, then prayed that the giant dog hadn't heard.

"Let's get back to our horses and ride for help," said Jon, trying to sound reasonable but obviously freaking out. We really needed to bring him along on more of our adventures so he could get used to this.

"No time," said Kestrel.

"But it's a good idea to get back to our horses," I said, a simple plan forming in my mind as I spoke. "Then I can distract the mustang hunters while you go get help."

"Jon can get help. I'll go with you."

"No, you get help," Jon said. "I'll go with Evy."

No matter how much I wanted to know that Jon liked spending time with me, I felt irritated. Now was not the time to argue. "Let's go."

*Rusty! Twilight!*

We crashed back through the bush, no longer concerned about the noise we made. Speed was the important thing now. I lost Jon and Kestrel when I went around the opposite side of a cluster of pine trees – and Rusty slid to a stop right in front of me. He humped his back when Twilight bumped into him from behind, threatening to kick. I launched into his saddle, then wildly looked around for Kestrel and Jon.

A bit of sky blue, Kestrel's jacket, flashed between distant trees. But I didn't need to talk to her – she'd know where I'd gone. Plus this seemed a good way to avoid their argument about who was coming with me. I leaned over Rusty's neck. "Let's go, buddy."

Rusty was off like a shot. As we careened through the forest, ducking branches and jumping over logs, I kept up a disjointed conversation with the two horses, explaining to them what I'd seen. The mustangs were loud and clear in my mind as well, their emotions rattling around my brain like ping pong balls. Some were mad, some confused. A couple were in pain. Every single one was frightened.

When Rusty asked me why they had captured the mustangs, I let a silence grow between us. How could I explain slaughter houses without making humans look like complete jerks? Nor would it do Rusty and Twilight any good to know places existed just to kill horses. I knew they'd understand that *I* would never hurt a horse, but honestly, I was embarrassed for my species.

We reached the road, and Rusty straightened into a fast gallop right down the middle of the dirt track, mud flying behind him. The ranch gates drew nearer and nearer. So close.

Too close. I hadn't figured out what I was going to say to the bad guys yet, and it had to be something good if it was going to delay the loading of the horses until help arrived. If only there was some way to communicate to the wild horses that going inside the truck was something they did *not* want to do.

Aha! My helper, Wildfire.

*Get out of truck*, I said as calmly as I could to Wildfire. No point in totally freaking her out by mind-yelling at her.

*Man in way!* Okay, so obviously she was already freaking.

*Get out! Fight if you have to!*

A loud bellow sounded. *Okay. Will fight.* Wildfire wasted no time. Banging sounds ricocheted past us, then yells. Wildfire was rearing up inside the back of the truck, totally spazzing.

Rusty quickly sidestepped to the sagging gate and I bent down to loosen the catch. The bolt slid back like it had been oiled. I pushed on the gate, expecting it to swing open like a normal ranch gate – but it went about a foot, dropped down, and hit the ground.

Wildfire bellowed again, both furious and terrified as she tried to battle her way back down the ramp and into the corral, pushing against the tide of horses coming up the chute at her. I didn't need to concentrate to know what she was feeling or seeing. The fear and panic from all the mustangs bombarded me like bullets. I could see them pushing up the ramp toward Wildfire more clearly than I could see the gate in front of me. One of the guys was behind them, yelling and stinging them with his long whip, over and over, and yet they couldn't escape. Wildfire was in front of them, acting like a mad thing, shoving against them, biting, striking, and fighting for all she was worth in her attempt to get out of the truck.

There was no calming this situation with mind tricks. The guy with the whip was going to be a lot more influential than any soothing thoughts I could send to them.

*Hurry!* Twilight said.

*Trying.*

*No try. Do.*

Okay, so when did my horse turn into Yoda?

I slipped from Rusty's back and threw my weight against the gate. It raked a couple of inches across the mucky ground. I shoved again and it slid a few more inches. It was going to take forever to get it open far enough that when I freed the mustangs, they could run out of the ranch yard.

Shove. Slide. Shove. Slide.

And then Twilight's bum was beside me and she was backing into the fence. Shove. Big slide. Shove. Biggest slide of all! Then Twilight wheeled away and trotted into the ranch yard.

*Wait*, I called after her, but she was having none of that. She was on her way to rescue her friends.

I climbed into Rusty's saddle, took a quick look back down the road – Kestrel and Jon were just reining their horses onto the dirt track. One of them would be here in less than a minute. Feeling much safer, I loped Rusty into the ranch yard.

Twilight had stopped at the corral fence and was peering over the high top rail. Her loud whinny dwarfed the general scuffling, squealing, and kicking sounds.

A horse exploded from the group of mustangs near the mouth of the chute, a dark foal on her heels. I almost died. Not Wind Dancer and her baby! But yes, it was them. And right behind her came Night Hawk, Twilight's sire. Then a black head rose above the throng and gazed about grumpily, looking suspiciously like Black Wing. Logic dictated that Ice was there too, just too deep in the herd to see.

Then suddenly, all thought of Twilight and her old herd flew from my mind – Twilight got a second response to her desperate neigh. The older man stalked toward my filly from inside the corral, scattering her herd back into the main mass of horses. As he marched, he yelled back to his son, standing near the horses at the chute. "One of them got out!"

"What? No way. How could one get out?"

The older guy said something back, but I wasn't listening anymore. I never wanted to hear a word this man said ever again – because I knew this guy. And now I understood why Wildfire had twice said "mean man." This man was indeed mean, and no one knew it better than the two of us. He was Wildfire's old owner, the one I had once saved her from.

In the instant that I recognized him, he saw me sitting there on Rusty. And he didn't take nearly as long to clue in as I had. He knew who I was within a fraction of a second; I could tell by the way his eyes turned hard as mirrors. A tight smirk crawled onto his face. He remembered our last deal all right, plus the fact that a mere girl had threatened him with exposure and made him look like a fool as he tried to sell a crazy horse to Jon for a lot of money – yes, that was Wildfire, but with an owner like him, she had some good reasons to act crazy.

I heard hoofbeats behind me and turned, expecting to see Kestrel *or* Jon. Instead I saw both of them, and both of them had their eyes locked on the older man. So no help was coming. It was just us against this horrible cruel man and his son.

"Need some help, Dad?" The shout came from the porch. Two more young guys stood there, glaring at us with hard eyes that looked exactly like their father's.

How many kids did this guy have?

As if on cue, the dog climbed to his paws from where he lay in the shade of the truck, and stalked toward Rusty and me, his lip curled up and a growl floating in front of him.

The dad's smirk grew into an evil smile. "I'm guessing the rescue squad has arrived," he drawled.

All three younger men laughed.

*Mean man*, Wildfire said again.

*Yes, mean man.* Really, what else could I say?

# Chapter 5

"Put that buckskin in with the others," the dad said to the two men on the porch, saying the words I least wanted to hear in the entire world. "She's looks like a wild one."

"She's mine!" I yelled. "Don't you touch her!"

But the two younger guys were already marching toward us and both were shaking out lassos, getting ready to throw them at Twilight.

"You got a bill of sale? Something to prove she's yours?" Mean Man asked as he climbed over the fence. On the ground again, he made a strange jerking motion with his head.

"I have people who can witness that she's mine."

Mean Man gestured to Jon and Kestrel. "Who? These two?" He nodded to his two advancing sons, and the son in front grinned back. What was going on? "I don't think these two are going to be much good to you for a while."

And then the lassos were flying – not toward Twilight but toward Kestrel and Jon! We'd been tricked.

"No! Leave them alone!" I screamed when the ropes settled around my two friends. And in that second, Mean Man rushed the last few steps to Rusty's head and grabbed his bridle. One more step, and he was pulling me from the saddle.

I'm not sure what happened then with Jon and Kestrel, not for a few seconds anyway. I fought and kicked and elbowed and bit and struggled with all my strength to free myself from Mean Man's iron grip –

and suddenly I was flying through the air. I hit the muddy ground and made a furrow with one shoulder, then pushed myself upright just in time to see my would-be captor racing for the truck. He wasn't running from me. He ran from Rusty and Twilight, both right behind him, and striking at his fleeing backside with the most vicious looks on their equine faces that I'd ever seen.

Where were Kestrel and Jon? Just before one of the two sons slammed the door to the cabin, I caught a glimpse of Kestrel's furious expression and Jon struggling to pull the rope over his head. The two sons stood on the porch, breathing heavily, and when they turned toward me, I could see that one of them had a bloody scratch down his cheek. Good for Kestrel!

Blam!

I screamed. Mean Man was leaning from the truck window with a rifle in his hands. A rifle pointed above Rusty's head. Life became slow motion as my beloved gelding jumped to the side.

Oh. My. Gosh.

*Run, Rusty! Run, Twilight! Back to woods!*

Without a moment's hesitation, my two horses leapt to a full gallop.

*No leave you*, said Rusty.

*Men will not hurt me. Only hurt you.* And I was almost completely certain of that. These guys were bullies and horse killers – they probably wouldn't physically harm me. They'd love to catch me and throw me in the cabin too though. I still had to keep out of their reach, if I was going to help the mustangs.

Twitchy and Cleo trotted slowly after Rusty and Twilight, like the calm saddle horses they were – far too slowly to actually escape if the men decided to catch them and ship them with the mustangs being sent to slaughter. I ran toward them, waving my arms; they picked up a little speed but they were still far too relaxed. They'd heard gun shots before, lots of times.

Rusty and Twilight were completely out of sight when I finally got them out of the ranch yard and jogging down the road. I stopped at the gate. It would be so easy to catch up to Twitchy, leap into her saddle, and gallop for help. Mom was just a few minutes away at a fast gallop. But that would mean leaving Kestrel, Jon, and the mustangs. How many could they load up while I was running off to find someone to help us? – when I could just stop all this myself.

If I did things right.

Whatever *right* was.

I turned back to face my enemies. Mean Man was climbing out of the truck cab, thankfully without his rifle. He must have stowed it back in its rack. Son Two and Son Three, the two guys that grabbed Kestrel and Jon, were walking back toward him, leaving the black dog on the porch to act as guard. And the dog was taking its job seriously; it stared at the crack in the door as Kestrel and Jon watched us, its lips pulled back in a snarl.

"So let's get them loaded." Son One, the first of the three sons I'd seen, was looking down from the back of the now empty truck. All of the mustangs were back in the corral. Wildfire had done her part of the rescue. Finally, something had gone right.

Son Three pointed to me. "Do you want us to put her with the others?" he asked, a little too eagerly for my tastes.

I poised to run.

Their old man looked at me, amused. "Naw," he finally said. "She can't do nothing now but waste our time. And I want her to see us load up these hayburners."

Son One and Son Two laughed, while Three looked disappointed. He was probably just as mean as his father. But not as smart. I could see that in his eyes. He was the kind of guy that took orders, not gave them.

But then the old man leaving me loose wasn't so smart either. And no way was a dog going to keep Kestrel and Jon locked inside a cabin. I glanced sideways. Sure enough, the dog had not only stopped growling, but was looking at the crack in the door with interest. Kestrel had to be feeding him goodies from the fridge; that's what I'd be doing anyway. The next thing Mean Man knew, his big, angry guard dog would be full and happy and probably snoring contentedly on the most comfy bed in the cabin, while Kestrel and Jon were free to create havoc. I smiled.

*What to do?* asked Twilight.

I zoned into her. She was just out of sight, standing with Rusty, Twitchy, and Cleo.

How could I utilize Twilight and Rusty's strengths?

And my plan fell into place. It wasn't an overly brilliant plan. There were lots of things that could go wrong and probably would – but at least we'd be doing something to help. One thing was for certain, doing nothing wasn't going to save any mustangs.

But before I told Rusty and Twilight to come back, I needed to make sure the ranch yard was safe for them.

Mean Man, One, and Three were inside the corral now. Two was behind the truck somewhere, or at least that's where he'd disappeared just moments ago.

Taking the few scraps of courage I had left, I jogged silently back toward the corrals. The men didn't seem to notice me as I moved deeper into the ranch yard; they were too busy trying to chase the mustangs toward the loading chute. My heart pounded like a mad thing as I drew even nearer. Any one of them could just glance in my direction, see me, and alert the others...

I desperately needed a diversion. If they saw me now and decided to catch me, I was too close to outrun them.

Wildfire was only too happy to oblige. Even I was shocked by how vehemently she rushed toward Mean Man and One, who happened to be standing near one other. The men dove in different directions and Wildfire rushed between them, her ears pinned and her eyes glaring. Now that she'd had her first victory over her old nemesis, she wanted more! She spun toward Mean Man again as he scrambled away from her – and then I stopped watching. Time to act.

Bending low, I raced the rest of the way to the truck. I reached the front grill just as Wildfire's scream of rage ripped the air. The thunder of hooves swelled around me as she got the rest of the mustangs moving.

I looked around the side of the truck. Two was nowhere in sight. He must've gone to help his dad and brothers. A moment later, I was opening the truck door.

No, I wasn't going to steal their truck. I didn't know how to drive, at least not safely, plus they had another old beat up pickup parked in front of the cabin and could've easily followed me. Besides, it's illegal to steal vehicles and I had no doubt Mean Man would press charges once I was caught, and I *would* be caught.

I had a better plan in mind. No one was going to drive the truck. Just as I hoped, the keys were in the ignition. I snatched them out, leaned across the filthy seat to lock the passenger door, then opened the driver's side door, locked it, slid out, and quietly shut the door, the keys still in my hand. Now they weren't going anywhere, plus the rifles were locked away. Ha! With one swift movement, I tossed the keys far beneath the truck. They'd have to get on their hands and knees to even look for them under there.

I glanced at the porch before hurrying to the front of the truck again. The dog was nowhere in sight. I almost laughed out loud. No doubt he was eating a lovely meal inside, while Kestrel and Jon had slipped out the door and were probably going for help. Wildfire had been more than a distraction for just my excellent plan.

I could've ditched my risky plan and followed Kestrel and Jon right then. It would have been easy. Let the guys load the mustangs; they weren't going anywhere with them. And we could collect enough help within half an hour to be back at the ranch in force. But there was one big problem. Leaving would mean abandoning Wildfire, the one who'd put herself at risk in order to cause a diversion. By now, the four men were probably super enraged by her actions. She might be in danger from them.

A moment later, my suspicions were confirmed. I peered around the front of the truck to see Wildfire totally freaking, rearing and slashing, trying to bite and kick, with all four men standing around her, yelling and cursing. The poor thing!

Then Mean Man's voice rose above the din. "Go get my bull whip!"

Son Three hustled toward the far side of the corral, in the direction of the ramshackle barn. Mustangs scattered before him like terrified mice. Their waves of panic rolled through my mind, obliterating all reasonable thought and making me want to run myself.

But I couldn't. Wildfire needed me. I forced the panic back. Now was the time to think and act, not simply react. Now was the time for my non-brilliant but potentially effective plan.

I'd noticed when I first saw the layout of the ranch that the corrals were like a warren, a maze of enclosures, alleyways, and squeeze chutes. Then, when I'd ridden Rusty into the ranch yard, I'd seen how completely confusing and extensive they were. One enclosure opened to another and another and another, all of the spaces smaller than the corral that held the mustangs now, and most of them having more than one gate.

My plan: open as many of the gates as possible and allow the mustang herds to scatter among the corrals and alleyways. And while I was opening gates into the maze, hopefully the guys would be trying to chase the mustangs back into the big corral, leaving the way open for Twilight to come along and do her specialty: open the big corral's gate and letting the mustangs into the big ranch yard, where they could escape. Then Rusty and his specialty: running in to save me.

So why wasn't this a *brilliant* plan? Because the men might catch me before I could open enough gates. Because Twilight might not get the main corral's gate open. Or if she did, one of the men might notice it was open and lock the mustangs in the smaller corrals. Or if the mustangs did escape the corrals and get into the ranch yard, they might not find the big gates leading to freedom.

But even if all these things went wrong, we might still win. It would take *time* for the men to catch me and get all the mustangs in the big corral again, all ready to load up – and given time, help would arrive, thanks to Kestrel and Jon.

I dashed around the front of the truck to the corral next to the mustang's enclosure and slipped through the fence, then crouched there, gasping, as I waited for the yells.

Silence. The men hadn't seen me? They hadn't seen me! Maybe because the mustangs were crowding against the fence beside me, blocking their view. The poor horses were obviously freaking out that I was so close to them, but they still didn't scatter. I was far less scary than the men crowding them toward chute – especially than Mean Man and his whip. Some of them had felt its sting before. Their memories of that were like a brand burned into my mind.

I ran through the empty corral, searching for a second gate to the mustang's enclosure. No, don't tell me. This was the only enclosure that didn't have two gates?

*Open gate*, asked Twilight, reading my mind.

*If not seen*, I replied. It would do no good to have Twilight caught by these men. They'd ship her to slaughter as fast as any of the mustangs.

*Not seen*, she responded eagerly. She was just dying to do something to help.

I reached a fence and slipped through. There it was; a nice big gate that I could open to the mustang's enclosure, allowing them to spill into the corral I was standing in – a small space, but certainly better than

66

nothing. The mustangs needed any and every way they could find to distance themselves from the men.

I ran to the gate and the mustangs pressing against it shifted away a few feet. Still somewhat shielded by mustang bodies, I grabbed the catch and jerked on it. It moved about an inch. Another lousy gate. Great. I jerked again.

*Man by gate*, said Twilight.

Quickly, I asked Wildfire to go after whoever was standing near the main gate. *Not so hard he climbs over*, I added, hoping I'd been fast enough and Wildfire hadn't already sent him scrambling over the gate to where he'd see Twilight for sure.

A squeal sounded, then hoofbeats thumped the ground. I zoned into Wildfire's vision. She was facing Son Two, giving him the evil eye. And he was scared. Quickly, he backed along the fence, away from the gate. Awesome! Maybe this *had* been a brilliant plan – if I could just get this blasted gate open.

Then I heard the hollow thunder of hooves on wood. Many hooves. The mustangs were going up the ramp into the truck! No!

I jerked on the catch again, desperately. The metal bit into my palm, making me want to cry out – but it was worth it. The catch moved back just far enough. The gate was free! With aching hands, I pulled it back.

*Escape this way*, I called to Wildfire, and jerked again. With a shriek, the hinges loosened and the gate swung wide.

I turned and ran, this time to the second gate in the corral. Mustangs burst into the open space behind me. The second gate opened like its bolt and hinges had been oiled daily, and I thanked my lucky stars as I ran into the second corral in the maze, eyes searching for the next gate to open.

There it was! I changed direction.

But I was only halfway across the empty space when the mustangs charged around both sides of me, their hearts drumming and heads high as they hunted for a way out. Then the few became a crowd, a crowd of jostling, muddy, very large bodies.

The leaders reached the gate, still closed in front of me, and turned back – and I was alone in the centre of the mustang whirlwind. I was the eye of the storm as the horses galloped around and around me, some just inches away, some bucking and kicking and squealing as they became caught up in the furor.

I knew it was just a matter of time but there was nothing I could do to stop it: a sorrel colt came a little too close, knocking me with his shoulder. I went spinning, then bounced off another horse that I didn't even see and fell to my knees in the mud.

Hooves pounded the ground all around me. I didn't dare move, let alone try to stand. Something rough scraped against my side, then thunked into the mud beside me. I cried out from the agony of an untrimmed hoof sliding off my ribs.

There was nothing to do but curl into fetal position, belly down, back up, with hands over my head and neck, as the ground trembled beneath that multitude of terribly sharp hooves. The thunder grew louder and louder and I kept thinking it would crescendo, but it only grew and grew and grew – and for the first time in my life, after all the adventures that I'd had and all the dangerous situations I'd been in, I wondered if I would survive.

# Chapter 6

The rumble grew less dense. Human yells rose above the thunder: Mean Man and his three grown sons. I could hear them again.

And then I could hear only individual hoofbeats. The horses were leaving. And so were the men. Their yells were growing more numerous, but farther away. They mustn't have seen me here, covered in mud.

Cautiously, I loosened my grip and raised my head to watch the last three mustangs rush out of the small corral.

We'd done it!

I leapt to my feet – and sagged down to my knees as my side erupted in pain. Gingerly, I put my hand beneath my muddy jacket to feel my shirt, wet and sticking to my side where the unshod hoof had raked against my ribs. Ow!

But enough about my injuries. I had to see what was happening with the mustangs.

I staggered back through the two smaller corrals. Where was Twilight? Quickly I zoned into her.

Oh, the lovely, glorious freedom! Not just from my beloved Twilight, but from all the freed mustangs as they raced along the dirt road, farther from civilization with every stride. She had shown the escaping mustangs the gate and now was leading them to safety. Already, they were very close to being out of range.

A totally unwelcome thought whispered to me – Twilight would come back, wouldn't she? Despite the fact that she felt so excited, racing with the huge herd, she'd still want to return to me, right? Despite the stroke of the wind and the stretch of her muscles and the feeling of *belonging* that was so heady? Despite galloping with horses that she understood, horses who were wild and smart and as tough as old boots, just like she was.

I know it totally showed Twilight my insecurities, but I couldn't stop myself from asking, *Come home?*

*No worries*. And then she was too far away.

So... did that mean she was coming home? Or that I shouldn't worry because she'd never forget me? That she'd be safe and happy living with the mustangs again?

Okay, I had to stop thinking like this. And besides, I had to get out of here safely myself.

I reached the main mustang corral, now wonderfully empty, and hurried to the gate, hanging at an angle. Some of the mustangs must have bumped the gate as they rushed through the narrow opening, breaking it. Repairs were needed before it would hold any more creatures against their will, something that made me feel happy – as long as the poor mustangs were okay.

I looked around the ranch yard. Had they all escaped? Were they all on their way back to the wild? It appeared so. A warm glow started in my heart.

*Rusty?*

*Here!* And he was, galloping in through the big ranch gates. I waved to him so he'd see me by the corral, and he ran even faster. A moment later, he skidded to a stop, sending a spray of mud around me. Not that I could get any dirtier. I probably looked like some long extinct swamp creature.

Rather than think words to him, I simply sent him intense gratitude, and felt like the sun had just come out as I basked in his inner relief at finding me safe in return. Then stiff, sore, and aching, I climbed into the saddle.

Rusty and I had just started toward the exit, when I heard a horse neigh. I reined him in. The neigh sounded again, from the direction of the cabin, and I turned just in time to see the horse trot into view from behind the neglected building.

Wind Dancer.

The palomino spun around and stared behind her as if seeing a ghost, then her loud whinny cut the air.

And her longing for her foal cut through my heart. *Butterfly!*

The dark filly burst from behind the cabin, and then suddenly she was tumbling head over heels, a rope tight around her neck. She landed hard on her side, and lay there for a moment as if stunned. Lassos flew from behind the cabin. Wind Dancer leaped away, just in time, and the ropes slid off her back to the ground.

"Let her go!" I screamed, hardly aware that Rusty and I were racing toward the filly as fast as he could run. We screeched to a halt as the men came into view, all four of them with expressions like thunderclouds.

Wind Dancer spun to face us, ears pinned, while Butterfly climbed shakily to her hooves. The mare shook her head at us. We weren't the bad guys here, but she didn't know that.

And then Three's lasso was flying through the air. It settled around Wind Dancer's neck as she focussed on Rusty and me. The rope tightened.

"Get her too," Mean Man yelled to Two, the only one who hadn't caught something yet.

With my heart in my throat, I spun Rusty away from them, looking back over my shoulder to see if we needed to duck any ropes. We didn't. By the time Two had thrown his lasso, we were out of range.

"Go shut the gate!" yelled Mean Man, not wasting a moment. Son Two sprinted forward, gathering his rope as he ran.

I wanted to cry as I pointed Rusty toward the gate. If only I could stay and save Wind Dancer and Butterfly. I would've done anything for them, if there was anything more I could do – but I knew there wasn't. Rusty and I had no choice, no other option. We had to escape ourselves, then find the help that hadn't yet arrived, and hope it wasn't too late when we got back.

Rusty easily kept ahead of Two as we cantered through the ranch gate and along the road. Yelling, not directed at us anymore but at the two mustangs, faded as we left the ranch behind, then the unpleasant noise was completely covered by the drumming of my brave gelding's hooves pounding the dirt, rhythmically and firmly. But even though I couldn't hear the yelling anymore, I could feel the effect it had on Wind Dancer and Butterfly. Pity for them spun through my mind, mixing with the anger and fear I could feel from them.

And then, as always, Rusty's steady presence began to calm me – enough that I recognized the fatigue in his step. He was so game and plucky, always doing his best no matter how tired he was. And he had a lot of very good reasons to be tired today. Not only had he run a race, winning it by taking the most difficult route, but he'd both chased and escaped horse thieves, and rushed in to save me. The poor guy.

*Not poor*. Rusty said, sounding the closest to irritated I'd heard in a while.

*Sorry.*

We hurried around a corner, then past a neighbouring ranch that seemed deserted. Another few minutes and another deserted ranch house, this time on the other side of the road. Everyone was at the rodeo. We rounded another corner – and saw three horses and riders up ahead, coming quickly toward us. Could it be?

"Mom!" I yelled as we galloped closer. The person on the tallest horse waved. It was her!

Rusty was covered with sweat and flecks of foam when we stopped.

Mom reined Cocoa to a halt. "What have you done to Rusty?"

Immediately, I felt a flash of anger. These were her first words to me, after all I'd been through? And besides, she was the one with secrets, not me. But anger wouldn't help Wind Dancer and Butterfly. "You have to come help them," I began.

"How did you get so filthy?"

I glanced at Kestrel, a little desperately. Where should I start?

"We haven't had time to tell her," Kestrel said, guessing my question. "What happened?"

"We freed them, all but two." I felt sick as I said it.

"Wow," said Jon, clearly impressed.

"Two what?" asked Mom.

"Mustangs. That's why you have to come. We have to save them from this horrible man. He's the one who abused Wildfire, and now he's got Wind Dancer and Butterfly."

Mom looked confused. "Who are Wind Dancer and Butterfly?"

I took a deep breath. There was no time to explain. We needed to save the mustangs, not hang around chatting.

"The guy who used to own Wildfire has been rounding up mustangs to sell for slaughter," said Kestrel, realizing I was nearing the end of my rope.

As she continued to answer Mom's questions, I tried to listen for the two frightened mustangs – but we were too close to the rodeo. All I heard was a cacophony of a hundred horse emotions and sensations, drowning out Wind Dancer's and Butterfly's voices.

Twilight was nowhere within sensing distance either. Was she still running, getting further and further from me with every stride? Was she saying goodbye forever to the bits I wanted to put in her mouth, the saddles on her back. Would she ever come—

"Evy!"

"What? Huh?"

"I said, what do you expect me to do?"

"About what?"

Mom looked completely exasperated. "About the mustangs."

"Free them." I mean, what else would I expect her to do?

"How?"

"I don't know. Talk to the guy. Make him see reason. He won't listen to us, but he has to listen to another adult."

"I don't know about that."

"But you have to try, Mom. Wind Dancer is Twilight's mom. We can't leave them to die. And even if he decides to train them instead of sell them for slaughter, what kind of life is that for either of them, especially Butterfly? She'd grow up hardly remembering anything about being a wild horse. And she'll end up not trusting humans, just like Wildfire. He's so mean."

Mom shook her head in defeat. "Okay, I'll try. But I want one of you to go get Charlie. If this guy doesn't listen to me, he might listen to Charlie."

"I'll go," Jon quickly volunteered. "Cleo's aching for a good run, so we'll get there the quickest."

I looked at him gratefully. I didn't want Rusty to do anymore running around today. And honestly, I was feeling a wee bit tired and sore myself. "Thanks."

Jon nodded. "See you soon."

Kestrel, Mom, and I rode our horses back toward the ranch at a slow lope, which was still faster than I wanted Rusty to go, but it couldn't be helped. Every moment that passed was more time the men had to hide Wind Dancer and Butterfly in some back field. And even though I'd be able to find them regardless because of my gift, with Mom along we'd have to stay within the rules. In other words, no trespassing. No sneaking around. No eavesdropping. None of that fun stuff.

It took far too long to arrive at the big ranch gates once again, and when we passed through, the place looked deserted. The corral gate still hung askew, and the truck was still parked with its back against the chute, looking as if it hadn't moved an inch. I hoped the rifle was still locked inside.

We heard a woof, and turned to see the black dog waddling down the porch steps, looking like he'd swallowed a basketball. I caught Kestrel's eye and she smirked.

"Good boy, Belch," Kestrel called. The dog's tail started whipping back and forth. His tongue lolled out as he walked toward her and he had the most contented look on his face I'd ever seen. "Belch?" I couldn't help but ask.

"Just be glad we called him Belch. He was making noises from his other end too," Kestrel replied.

"Fun."

Kestrel wrinkled her nose. "You have no idea."

The door opened and Mean Man, followed by all three sons, stepped out onto the porch. Immediately, my mirth died. They looked far angrier and even nastier than before, something I'd thought impossible until now.

Mean Man swaggered down the stairs, his eyes looking harder than a snake's. Sons One, Two, and Three copied him. I almost laughed when Son Three descended. His knees were too far apart and he swayed back and forth just like a duck.

The father reached us. "To what do I owe the pleasure?" Though his words were polite, there was no mistaking the threat behind them.

"My girls say you're holding a couple of mustangs here."

"Ain't no mustangs here."

"Yes, that's what we said," Kestrel interjected.

"What?" Mean Man looked confused.

"If there aren't *no* mustangs here," I explained, "Then there must be at least one."

Mean Man stared at me, still not comprehending.

I raised my hands. "A double negative?"

Mom regained control of the conversation. "We want to see them."

"I told you, there ain't no mustangs here," said Mean Man, crossing his arms firmly across his chest.

I glanced at Kestrel and raised an eyebrow. She nodded – and then started to talk. I'm not sure what about because I faded into horse-land pretty quick, but I did hear something about how natural it is for miscommunication to occur when improper grammar is used.

I felt Wind Dancer and Butterfly immediately, and oddly enough, they were neither in the barn nor in the direction of the corrals. They were near the back fence, in the old sheds. But a single glance at the old buildings told me that was impossible. The sheds were falling to pieces; some didn't even have roofs anymore. They'd never hold a mustang, especially in complete and total darkness – for that's where Wind Dancer and Butterfly were, in absolute darkness, like the kind you find in caves.

Butterfly stood frozen on the spot, legs apart and head down as if she was afraid she was going to drop into an abyss at any moment, while Wind Dancer shuffled around on tiny excursions. Her sense of smell lead the way as she crept through spider webs and bumped into things in the dark, trying to nose out a bit of fresh air, searching for a way out for her and her baby.

I reined Rusty in their direction.

"Evy?" Mom said. "Where are you going?"

I turned back in the saddle as Rusty continued to walk. "They're over here."

"Go ahead. Look all you want. There's nothing in that shed," said the man.

I reined Rusty around the sheds.

"Wait!" he yelled.

Rusty increased speed to a trot. Behind the shed, there was nothing but a grassy mound and the back fence. On the other side of the fence, the dark forest spread away, thick and untouched. Was another building hiding in the trees? Rusty trotted up the bump in the grass, and I stopped him at the top, then peered into the shadows beneath the branches. I could see nothing suspicious in there, no glimmer of light against a board, no trail, not even an open space. Had my horse radar led me astray? I didn't think so. The two mustangs felt so near, it was like I should be able to touch them if I just reached out my hand.

Mean Man and his henchman stormed around the shed toward me, arms swinging, and not looking nearly as collected as they had just moments ago. This was proof my horse radar was right on. Why would the mustangs' captors look so worried unless I was basically right on top of them?

And then I got it. I *was* right on top of them. There was only one thing unique about this spot. The mound. It had to be a root cellar. People sometimes dug big holes, built their root cellar in the hole, and then covered them with the dirt.

Now all that remained was to find the door, wrench it open, and free the two mustangs.

But the men had arrived, looking madder than wet bobcats. There was no time to find the door, let alone open it. Mom and Kestrel rode behind them, Mom looking puzzled as she watched me. No doubt my actions seemed very strange to her, taking off in the middle of a conversation to dart around an old shed and then standing on top of a mound of grass. Only Kestrel looked normal, like she totally understood what was going on – but then she'd probably clued in that the mustangs were inside the root cellar the second she saw the grassy mound.

Mean Man crossed his arms across his chest and turned to Mom. "I want you off my property now, and your brats too."

Mom didn't say a word as she stared at him, but she didn't have to for me to see what was going on in her head. Her jaw was hardening, her eyes narrowing. I could practically see steam coming out of her ears, she was so instantly mad. Up to now, she'd been polite, even apologetic, but no more. Mean Man had just made a terrible blunder. He'd called Kestrel and me brats. Bad move, buddy – and time for me to just sit back and enjoy the show.

"If my daughter said there are mustangs here, there are mustangs here," she snapped. "And I expect you to be a man and not some weasely coward and admit it."

"Now, you—"

"These girls wouldn't lie to me. They are the most honest people I know. But *you*. I saw that mare Evy brought home last year. She was terrified of people, simply terrified."

"But I—"

It was hard to hold back my smile. He had no idea how long she could go on when she wanted to.

"I should have gone to the SPCA right then and there," Mom continued, her voice sharp as a razor. "I don't know why I didn't. But I can tell you this, if you don't hand over those mustangs right now, I am on my way to call them right now."

"Now hold on—" He was holding his hands out toward her in the stop position, desperately trying to slow her down.

"And another thing, what did you do to these girls to make them so upset? What did you say to them? You better not have touched them. Did he touch you, Evy? What did he say to you?"

Nervousness smeared across Mean Man's face like a toddler's breakfast. I raised an eyebrow at him. Should I tell?

"Maybe I should call the police while I'm at it," Mom said, not waiting for my answer. "They'll get to the bottom of this."

"Let's not be—"

"Hasty? You want to see hasty? You have two seconds to tell me if you have any mustangs on this property. That's it. Two seconds, or I'm riding out of here to get the police." Her hand shot toward the grassy mound, her finger pointing at Rusty's hooves. "And now you have one second left to tell me you have mustangs trapped in that root cellar that Evy finds so interesting."

That did it. I couldn't keep my face straight any longer. I even laughed. Go, Mom!

"What you gonna give me for them?"

"What do you mean?"

"That mare might be a good saddle horse someday."

"He isn't going to train her, Mom," I said. "He was going to sell her for slaughter."

"Now that don't make any sense," he said, turning to me. "It's not worth shipping just two of them. I'm going to break them. Sell them."

And I believed him. I could see it in his eyes. In fact, he *wanted* to keep Wind Dancer now so he could break her to ride as cruelly as possible – and he was just the kind of sick person who would enjoy taking out every speck of his anger on an innocent horse.

"Evy?"

I looked up at Mom.

"I'll give you five hundred for the pair," she said, instantly reading my expression.

Mean Man laughed. "Twenty five hundred." His sons all smiled behind him, as if they were puppets with the same strings tied to their lips.

"They're not worth that," Mom said, obviously flustered.

"Nope," Mean Man agreed.

"A thousand," said Mom. "Cash."

My mouth dropped open. She had that much money with her?

"Twenty five."

"Twelve fifty."

"Twenty five." The man shook his head, a smirk planted firmly on his face.

"Fifteen hundred."

Mean Man shook his head.

"Seventeen hundred," Mom said. "But that's it. Not one cent more." To accentuate that her decision was made, she backed Cocoa a step or two as if she was getting ready to leave. "And if I remember right, it's illegal to be cruel to animals. You have them locked in that root cellar and if that isn't cruel, I don't know what is."

Mean Man's smirk dropped from his face.

"Plus we'll testify that you had a whole bunch of mustangs here," I added.

"Yeah," said Kestrel, "And that you were being cruel – and not only to them."

"What do you mean, Kestrel?" asked Mom, her voice sharp again.

"Seventeen fifty," Mean Man said, suddenly sounding reasonable.

"Evy, what did Kestrel mean by that?"

Okay, so now I was in a tough spot. I couldn't lie because of Rusty, but I couldn't tell Mom that the guys had thrown Kestrel and Jon into their cabin as prisoners or that I'd been jerked from Rusty's back. If I did, Mom would be off Cocoa's back in a flash, yelling hysterically in his face, and then who knew what bad things might happen? But there was one other option. "He's mean to his dog. You saw how it could hardly move."

Rusty switched his tail, but that was all. Maybe he recognized that I was trying to protect the extremely fragile peace. Kestrel gave me a small thumbs-up that Mom couldn't see, and tried not to smile.

"So as soon as you have the money in cash, come back," Mean Man said, feeling confident again. "Maybe I won't have changed my mind."

Mom pulled an envelope from her saddlebag. "I'll give it to you now."

Mean Man's eyes almost popped out of his head when she took a wad of bills from the envelope. Cautiously, he approached Mom who was sitting high on Cocoa's back, then reached for the money.

She jerked it out of his reach. "Turn them loose first."

"Don't you want a halter?"

"What do you think?" she said in a way that really said, 'You're an idiot.'

Mean Man shrugged, then signalled to Son One. As the young guy hustled around the side of the mound, I rode Rusty to stand beside Mom and Kestrel.

Son One groaned, hinges shrieked, and then there was a loud "Hey!"

Wind Dancer burst into view, all cream and gold and vibrant motion. Mom gasped in delight, her hands flying to her heart. Butterfly appeared, blinking in the light, then bumped into her mother as Wind Dancer stopped to stare at us. A moment later they were off again, Butterfly stuck like a dark burr to Wind Dancer's heels as they raced away.

Money flew through the air, tumbling around us like autumn leaves. Mom stuffed the envelope into her saddlebag, then spun Cocoa toward the gate. Kestrel and I galloped our horses right behind her. I only looked back once – and saw two of the men snatching dirty money out of the mud while the others ran after bills caught in the breeze.

We raced after Wind Dancer and Butterfly, and of course, they were petrified of us, which made it easy to herd them toward the gate. Once through, they ripped down the dirt road, kicking up clods of dirt and mud as they ran in the same direction the other mustangs had gone.

Mom, Kestrel, and I pulled our horses to a stop on the road and watched them race away. Quickly, I zoned into Twilight. Yes, she was in range. Had she been coming back to find me?

*Wind Dancer and Butterfly coming your way.*

Twilight responded immediately. *Will take home.*

*See you later at our home?*

*Yes.*

I almost cried with relief. I know it was silly, being so worried, but Twilight and I had been going through our "bit" battle for a while, and I knew she was as sick of it as I was. In some ways, I wouldn't have been too surprised if she'd decided to take a break out in the wild.

Hoofbeats sounded behind us, forcing me to collect my emotions. A moment later, I turned to face Charlie and Jon, for I'd guessed that was who was riding up behind us. Both of them looked worried when they reached us.

"I'll go talk to them," Charlie said, after hearing the story. "But tell me first, how much did he charge you for the two?"

"It doesn't matter. What matters is that they're safe now," Mom said, firmly.

Charlie nodded, respecting her decision to keep the information private. "And I'll make sure of that. Time for Spriggs to know I'm watching him."

Ah, so that was Mean Man and his sons' last name: Spriggs. I wouldn't be forgetting it.

Charlie reined his big red horse through the ranch gates.

"Hey, Charlie."

He looked back at me.

"You mind getting us a Bill of Sale? And maybe one from the purchase of Wildfire last year too?" You never know, they might come in handy in the future.

Charlie nodded.

I glanced at the cabin. Spriggs was standing on the porch now, arms crossed. Belch lay at his feet, stretched out fast asleep, his stomach huge and round. "You want us to wait for you?" I added.

"No, you go on and have some fun. I hear you have a prize to collect." He winked, then rode into the ranch yard.

"A prize to collect?" asked Mom.

"Um, yeah. I was going to tell you about that," I stammered.

"What did you do?"

Now why would she sound so suspicious? "Nothing. Just a race, that's all."

"Ah, the Barrel Race. You won again?" She sounded happy for me, proud even.

"Um, not quite..."

# *Chapter 7*

It took a while to explain it to Mom, and though we did most of the explaining as we rode back to the rodeo, we still arrived too late for any of the gymkhana games. No additional prize money this year.

Mom hung around until I collected the money for the Downhill Mountain Race, though not in obvious sight. She was extremely shy of people. After I got the cash, I met her behind the General Store and gave it to her. She took it silently, a pensive expression on her face. "You don't have to do this, Evy. You can keep the money if you want."

"No, I want to, Mom. Really."

She hesitated. "Taking care of our family isn't your job, sweetheart," she said softly.

"But this just barely covers what you just spent."

"And fifty dollars more. At least take that."

I shook my head. "I want to help out. I'm not a little kid anymore."

"No, that you are not." Mom reluctantly slipped the cash into the envelope, then stuffed it in her saddlebag.

"So that was lucky, you having that much money with you," I said, doing a little fishing for information.

She didn't say a word as she took off her jacket. Maybe if I was more direct?

"So why *did* you have that much money with you? And what were you doing in town?"

"I had to see someone about something," she answered, holding out her jacket to me.

Okay, so that told me absolutely nothing. "Was it the sales of the spring paintings?"

She nodded. "One of them sold," she said, deciding to throw me an obvious tidbit of information.

"But you had less than two thousand dollars. They're worth a lot more than that."

Mom pushed her coat closer to me. "I'll take your muddy coat home with me," she said cheerfully, totally ignoring my comment. "You can wear mine."

I recognized that cheer. It meant fake-Mom was back. And I suddenly felt ridiculously happy. She hadn't been able to do fake-Mom for a while; for far too long, morose-and-silent-Mom had reigned.

"Thanks," I said, removing my mucky coat. My pants were filthy too and I had mud in my hair, but I'd try to clean that up at the river before going back to the rodeo.

Mom tied my muddy coat behind her saddle. "See you soon," she said, and asked Cocoa to walk on. She looked back. "Remember to get home before dark."

"I'll remember." I waved and she waved back, then I watched her ride away, feeling frustrated. What did she think she was saving me from? Knowing she had this mysterious and possibly dangerous past? Kind of knew that already. Knowing I had family in Vancouver, including possibly the scariest grandmother that ever existed? Knew that too. Finding out who Tristan, he of the mysterious birth certificate, was? Okay, so that I didn't know. Nor who she'd met in town today. The only thing I could guess was that the person she'd met had gotten the rest of the money she'd made from the sale of that painting. Again I wondered if it was a private investigator.

Slowly, I rode back to the rodeo. After I cleaned up a bit, there wasn't much to do, except hang out with Jon and Kestrel, tell jokes, pig out on greasy rodeo food, and let Rusty rest before our long walk home.

I found my two friends already getting a head start on the pigging out part. After tying Rusty beneath a tree for shelter, taking off his saddle, and giving him some water, I joined them with my very hungry stomach. Funny how running races, being nabbed by bad guys, and rescuing mustangs can build up an appetite.

Half an hour passed under a big tent in fast food heaven. Not healthy, and I felt totally gross after, but it sure tasted good going down. We traded stories, them telling me about feeding poor Belch the best meal of his life, then escaping and the mad hunt for Cleo and Twitchy.

I told them about locking the truck and dispersing the mustangs among the corrals while Twilight opened the gate to the ranch yard.

"You mean she *knew* to sneak up behind them and open the gate?"

"Um, yeah. She's like really smart."

"And then she ran off with the wild ones."

"Yeah." No way was I going to mention that she came back and then led Wind Dancer and Butterfly back to their range.

"But, how do you know? I mean, she could've just been running off. You can't know where she was taking them."

Good point. "Uh, I was just guessing?"

"Gotta go, guys," said Kestrel, being no help at all – and then she was up and moving toward someone waving at her from across the rodeo grounds.

There was a long silence in which I thought frantically of something smart to say. Nothing came to mind.

"You're pretty good with horses," Jon finally said.

"Not really," I said, suddenly feeling super shy.

Our eyes caught. Jon blushed. I looked down, then picked at a fry.

Jon cleared his throat.

"You want to go check on Rusty and Cleo?"

"Sure," I said, relieved. Rusty always made me feel more confident. I stood, inhaling sharply when my clothes rubbed against my scraped ribs.

"You okay?"

"Yeah," I said and nodded. "I just got bumped by one of the mustangs." No point mentioning that its hoof had slid off my ribcage, taking a fair amount of skin with it. I mean, that was just gross.

Rusty greeted us with a whinny. He was feeling much better after his rest.

"He's an amazing horse," said Jon, running his hand along Rusty's neck.

"Yeah, I wish you could have seen the whole race. There was this one time, when a bay gelding kept cutting him off..." And we were off and running with the conversation. No more not knowing what to say. There was just one quiet moment: when I straightened Rusty's mane and Jon's hand touched mine. I felt like I'd been zapped with electricity and I think he felt the same because he stopped talking in mid-sentence and looked into my eyes.

No question about it. He still liked me.

"Do you think you can come out to see Twilight this summer?" I asked, feeling just a little disconnected with reality. "Maybe you can help me with her training."

"I'll come out next week," he said, his blue, blue eyes locked on mine.

"Hey, guys!" Kestrel was back.

We got back to the joking and teasing for the last few minutes before we left, and then Kestrel and I were on our way. I looked back once and was happy to see Jon still watching us ride away. When I waved, he waved back.

"Okay, tell me *everything*," said Kestrel, wasting no time. "And start at the beginning with the details about what happened with the mustangs, right to the end."

"The end?"

Kestrel grinned. "You and Jon, of course. It was torture hanging out with Christy. All she does is talk about how cool she is. But I sacrificed myself just for you two."

"Okay, from the beginning..."

Thank goodness there was so much exciting stuff to talk about that Kestrel didn't have time to ask me anything about Mom before we reached her place. I really didn't want to talk about that yet, not until I had time to think about it first and figure things out a little. Kestrel and I waved goodbye to each other when we reached her big ranch gates, then Rusty and I meandered the rest of the way home.

It was lovely arriving just at sunset. The clouds had thinned further since mid-day, and the sky glowed vermillion and peach as the sun dropped near the horizon. Cocoa was in the pasture beside the barn, shining in the evening light.

Loonie rose to her feet when Rusty and I rode into the yard. Rascal wasn't quite so sedate, zooming toward us like a furry bullet. He bounced up and down beside Rusty, a big grin on his face, and I couldn't help but laugh. Mom came out on the porch and waved. It felt so good to all be together again – except for Twilight. I sent out my horse radar. Yes, she was here too, down by the lake. My heart smiled as Rusty hustled toward the barn with a little more spring in his step.

Twilight trotted around the side of the cabin, her legs glistening wet from wading as she caught up to us. Her satisfaction and feeling of all being right with the world told me more than anything that Wind Dancer, Butterfly, and the others were safe. Though some of the mustangs might still have great distances to travel to return to their ranges, they were all alive. They were all free.

Inside the barn, I unsaddled Rusty, being careful not to bump my ribs as I pulled it from his back. Free of the weight, he groaned and stretched. I plopped the saddle on the ground and moved to massage his back. Because I could feel what he felt, I knew what spots hurt him and what areas felt good to be massaged, and as my fingers worked the soreness away, the echo of his pain slowly eased in my own back.

Twilight waited for almost fifteen minutes before she began to bug me for her grain. First, it was impatient sighs, then stompings. Finally, she bumped my shoulder. Cocoa looked up eagerly from where she waited in her stall. She'd come inside the second we'd entered the barn, knowing oats would be arriving sometime. Now, because of Twilight's impatience, she knew they were imminent.

"You're a pest," I said to my filly, and ruffled her forelock. She nickered to me, then nuzzled my bumped shoulder, as if to kiss it better.

"Okay, let's get the oats." I hung Rusty's bridle and Twilight's halter and rope over the saddle horn, then carried everything to the feed/tack room. Twilight stood in the doorway as I set out the buckets, watching every move I made.

I had just moved to the cupboard to get their vitamin mix, my back to the door, when I heard movement behind me. Twilight sure was impatient tonight. But when I turned back around, she wasn't nosing the buckets, trying to sneak some grain. She was tugging on her bridle.

Wow, she hated that bridle so much that she wanted to eradicate its presence, even as it hung innocently in the tack room?

The headstall came loose from its hook and fell to the floor. One hoof came up, paused, and then gently lowered. Twilight bent her head and gingerly took the bit in her teeth, then lifted the bridle from the ground.

What was going on?

And then my filly sent me the saddest sensation I'd ever felt from her: how she felt when things were exciting or scary, and I wasn't able to hear her because I'd shut down my horse radar.

Alone. Cut off. Abandoned.

I put down the vitamins and hurried toward her. She released the bit into my hand and with a look of supreme distaste on her face, opened her mouth. She wanted to learn to use the bit so I could still communicate with her when we weren't able to talk with our thoughts.

Tears studded my eyes and I threw my arms around her neck. She was so special, so wonderful, so giving. She loved me enough to do this thing that was so horrible to her.

And I loved her enough that I would never ask her to wear the bit again.

*Have better idea*, I told her.

I hung the bridle up again, then grabbed her halter from where it still hung on Rusty's saddle horn. Why hadn't I thought of this before? I unclipped the lead rope, then removed the reins from the bridle and reattached them to the halter.

*Use this instead*, I said, holding up the halter, a rein attached to each side of the noseband. Other people would accept that she could be ridden with just a halter, and though they might think it unusual and maybe even outright strange, I didn't really care about that. What I *did* care about was them thinking I was doing something impossible, because then they'd suspect my gift – but being directed by a comfy halter with reins wasn't impossible. It would only make Twilight look very obedient and well trained.

I smirked. The words Twilight and obedient didn't seem like they should go in the same sentence.

Twilight's approval flowed into me as she understood what I was trying to tell her, and she reached forward to nuzzle me. I dropped the halter to the ground and stroked her face as we basked in our mutual feelings of the other's awesomeness for a few tender moments.

Then she bumped me with her nose. Enough with the mushy stuff. Time to eat.

The next day dawned, beautiful and clear. It had rained a bit more during the night and now everything lay washed and clean, sparkling in the morning sun.

Mom still wasn't up when I went out to the barn to see the horses, Rascal bouncing at my heels. I was kind of glad she was still sleeping. Though she'd been as irritating as usual with her secrets yesterday, our relationship had still healed a little. Her saving the mustangs and acting more normal, or more normal for her, had gone a long way. And I know it's weird, but even though I knew I missed her before yesterday, I hadn't realized how much until I got a little bit of her back – and if I was just going to lose her all over again, I wanted to put it off as long as possible.

Rusty was in his stall, still sound asleep, when I walked into the barn. I quietly prepared their morning grain and when I came out of the feed/tack room, all three horses were looking eagerly over their stall partitions at me.

But while Twilight and Cocoa dove into their oats with gusto, Rusty lowered his head slowly. My muscles ached as he shuffled closer to the bucket. Poor guy.

*Not poor.*

Oops.

I gave them all a good grooming, spending extra time with Rusty, hoping to ease his aching muscles. I think the steady pressure of the brush helped but nothing was going to have as much effect as a couple of days of rest. And he certainly deserved it after all he'd done yesterday.

When I was afraid that his skin might start feeling tender because of too much brushing, even with the soft bristles, I switched to just using my hands and rubbing his muscles and back. Rusty groaned and shifted whenever I hit a tender spot, but most of the time, he stood with his bottom lip twitching in pleasure, his eyes half closed and dreamy.

*Time to go*, said Twilight, when my arms felt like they were about to fall off.

*Go?*

*Where family caught.*

93

I stopped massaging Rusty. Twilight had found the corral that the Spriggs family had built to capture mustangs? Probably yesterday as she was gallivanting about with the various herds. This was amazing news! And definitely something I needed to act on, sooner rather than later.

But Rusty needed rest.

*Me*, said Twilight.

At first I didn't understand what she meant. She told me again.

I didn't want to insult her, but did I *dare* ride Twilight to find the corrals? It would mean heading off into the wilderness on a horse that had never been ridden before and that I could guide only with my thoughts. In other words, she could choose to ignore me, as she regularly did at least once a day, and I'd be at her mercy. Even if she had some knowledge of how reins worked, that would be something.

Maybe if she would accept a saddle...

*No.*

Okay, so without a saddle too. And did I mention the "into the wilderness" part?

And then I realized that Twilight felt nervous too. Heading off on a long trek, wearing a halter with reins, with a human on her back was really scary to her. What if I wanted her to do something she didn't want to do? What if I became overbearing and forceful if I didn't get my way?

And suddenly I knew my fears were as meaningless as Twilight's. Ours wasn't the normal relationship between horse and human, where communication lines were dependent on physical touch. We were friends. We were partners. We knew what the other was thinking. We could even talk to each other.

But most important of all, we could *listen* to each other.

All of a sudden, I felt only excitement. My first ride on Twilight! I'd waited years for this.

I said goodbye to Rusty with a snuggle, then haltered Twilight, tied the ends of the reins together and laid the knot on her neck so I wouldn't be tempted to use the reins too much. My old mounting block was where I'd left it years ago, in the corner of the feed/tack room. I moved it to Twilight, then stepped up and put my hands on her back, and paused.

My heart was thudding worse than when I'd run the Downhill Mountain Race or touched Jon's hand, and I felt like I was glowing with exhilaration. Twilight was excited too. I felt the thrill of the momentous occasion coursing through her body. Tiny tremors vibrated beneath my hands, like there was an electrical current right underneath her warm, silky skin.

Just do it!

I gave a little hop and put my weight on her back, then slid my right leg over her hindquarters, and straightened.

I was riding Twilight! Her ears were back so she could hear me better, and her head was turned slightly, so she could watch me with one eye. Slowly, almost reverently, I stroked her neck.

*Okay?* I asked.

Twilight snorted, then stamped a hoof. Obviously not that okay. I opened myself further to her struggle and almost wanted to buck myself off. For countless generations, wild horses had fought tooth and hoof to rid themselves of creatures who jumped on their backs. It was inbred in them so strong that it was almost an unfightable urge.

Thankfully, Twilight was fighting it.

*Will get off*, I offered. Actually, as the seconds passed and she didn't give in to the urge to send me flying, I was feeling more and more confident that she'd eventually let me ride her for real anyway, so getting off earlier than planned today wouldn't be a failure. I could always walk out to the corrals.

*Wait*, she replied.

I waited. And as I sat there, stroking her neck, she slowly, ever so slowly, almost imperceptibly slowly, relaxed. Then she started to walk. It caught me by surprise, and I clutched at her mane. The urge to pitch me off rose up again, but she pushed it down once more. We walked out of the barn and Twilight turned toward the cabin. Since she was the one who knew which direction the corrals lay, I didn't do anything but sit there. Rascal came dashing over from where he'd been very busily sniffing in the field, and sniffed at Twilight's back heels.

"No, Rascal," I said firmly, afraid Twilight would lose the little bit of control she had and kick him.

Twilight humped her back.

"Rascal!"

He darted away, then rushed around in front of us. Twilight relaxed again, much more quickly this time.

Even relaxed, she felt weird to ride. She was much narrower than Rusty, and her step wasn't as firm – probably because she wasn't used to my weight on her back yet. Also, the ground was further away than when I rode Rusty.

As we moved closer to the cabin, Mom came into view through the big front window. She was still in her pyjamas, seated in front of one of her blank canvases.

But wait! There were lines on it.

Mom was staring at the canvas like it was the most fascinating thing she'd ever seen, and as I watched she flicked a few more quick, light lines on the canvas with her paintbrush. She was sketching out her next painting? This truly was a miraculous day.

"Mom!"

Twilight jumped. I patted her neck with one hand, my way of saying sorry, and put my other hand over the reins on Twilight's neck. That way, it would look like I was holding them without me actually picking them up.

Mom looked out the window, her eyes unfocussed. Wow, she was in major artist land – awesome! And then she understood what she was seeing. Her mouth dropped open, and she jumped up, then disappeared from view as she moved to the front door.

*Stop*, I said.

Twilight stopped immediately. I was impressed. Maybe this really was going to work.

The front door burst open and Mom rushed outside. "You're riding Twilight? When did you start riding Twilight?"

"I've been working on her training for a while," I said, instantly falling into my old pattern of not answering the question that had actually been asked. And something inside me revolted. Twilight's bravery today as she fought her old patterns had affected me more than I could have guessed. My filly had acted the way she *truly wanted* to act, not the way that simply came natural to her. She hadn't thrown me sky high when I slid onto her back. And maybe I could say what I really wanted to say. "But honestly, this is our first ride," I added. An odd, transcendent calm washed over me.

"Amazing. She looks so relaxed. And you're riding her with just a halter? And bareback?" Mom looked up at me with a new respect in her eyes. "You really do have a gift, Evy."

"Twilight and I understand each other."

Mom walked down the steps to Twilight's head, then stroked her gold and ebony face. "It's hard to believe that she was born a mustang when I see her standing here like this."

"Yeah," I said, though to me it wasn't that hard to believe, maybe because I knew what Twilight was thinking most of the time. Some of her thoughts were pretty wild and crazy.

"Especially after seeing that mustang mare yesterday, Twilight's dam," Mom continued. "That's what Twilight would be like, if you hadn't tamed her."

I could have said that I wasn't sure who had tamed who when it came to me and Twilight. Or point out that Wind Dancer was actually a very reserved and calm mare for a mustang. But instead of saying these things, again I decided to say what I really wanted to say. And quick, before the strange calmness disappeared.

"Hey Mom, what else were you doing in town yesterday? I know you said you were picking up money from the sale of that painting, but I know you met with someone too, someone driving a black convertible."

Mom's face blanched white.

My mellow feeling grew deeper. "I know you won't tell me I'm right, and that's okay. All I ask is that you at least tell me if what I say is wrong." I cleared my throat to give myself time to compose my thoughts. "I think you gave most of the money from the painting to the person you met, and I think that person might be working for you, investigating things for you."

Mom sat down on the porch steps, looking stunned – but she wasn't denying anything.

"I think you've had this private detective hired all spring and summer to check out some people from your past. That's what's been in the brown envelopes you got in the mail, information about those people. And I think the investigation is costing a ton of money and that's why we're broke."

I paused to give her a chance to respond. She didn't. Instead, she wrapped her arms around herself, and looked so small and lost sitting there, staring down at the ground, that I stopped speaking.

I could have easily added that this investigator was collecting information for her about either her family or my dad's family – either way, *my* family – and that I had a right to know what that information was. I could've asked her outright who Tristan was, or why she was hiding from my grandmother. I could've asked her anything I wanted because for the first time in my life, I was feeling strong enough to say it all.

But seeing her sitting there, feeling alone and under attack, I recognized something more important than knowing the answers to my questions. I saw my mom, scared and in turmoil. She was just finding herself again after a terrible, unknown shock last spring. She'd just gotten out her paints and actually started to sketch. What right did I have to shake her out of that?

"And I just want you to know that I don't mind," I added, even though that wasn't totally true. Good thing I wasn't riding Rusty.

Mom looked up at me, tears lingering in her surprised eyes.

"I trust you to do what's right for us. If you need to gather information, that's okay with me," I said simply. And that part was true.

Mom stood. "Thanks, Evy," she croaked, her voice full of emotion.

"Just tell me about it sometime, okay? Sometime soon?"

She nodded, her lips pinched together like she was afraid that if she relaxed them, every secret she had would spill out that second.

"Twilight and I are going looking for the corrals the Spriggs built to capture the mustangs. We'll be back in a few hours," I added.

And to show how much Mom trusted me and my mustang filly, she didn't say a word about riding an untrained horse into the wilderness. Either that or she still was having trouble speaking.

*Go to corrals*, I said to Twilight, and my lovely filly started to walk. "Have fun painting," I called back to Mom and fervently wished she had returned to her old creative self. We certainly needed the money her paintings would bring – but even more important, she needed to paint to be happy. Her art fed her soul, just like Rusty and Twilight and the wilderness fed mine.

She waved silently to me, then turned toward the cabin door, and by the expression on her face, I could tell she was already thinking about her new painting again. Wonderful!

Rascal only hung out at the door for a millisecond before he was running after me and Twilight, quickly becoming our miniature shadow. Loonie watched us ride away, her head high. I wondered if she was hoping I'd call her, like I used to do. But she couldn't come with us today. It was probably a long way to the corrals, too far for Loonie to walk these days.

My guess was right. About six or seven miles into the bush, we came across poles nailed to trees. Twilight and I followed the single line of fence poles until we saw more poles nailed to trees on our other side, moving closer, forming a big funnel.

Finally, we came to the corral, conveniently situated for the mustang hunters at the end of a narrow, rutted logging road. There was even a chute, built to load the mustangs onto a truck.

And we were not alone. Charlie was there, ripping down the corrals. He must have gotten the location from the Spriggs when he talked to them yesterday.

When he saw me ride into the clearing on Twilight, he raised his eyebrows but didn't say a word. I slipped from Twilight's back, removed her halter, and then got to work beside him as she wandered over to flirt with Redwing. I didn't need to explain anything to Charlie about riding Twilight. He'd guessed my secret gift last year.

We worked side by side all morning and part of the afternoon, telling each other stories, laughing, joking, and talking about mustangs and other horses we knew, until the chute, corral, and funnel had been totally dismantled, the nails pulled, and the poles scattered.

Twilight was nowhere to be seen when we finished. While Charlie saddled Redwing for their ride home, I mind-called her.

*Busy. Back soon.*

I didn't mind; it was a great day out, peaceful and warm.

When Charlie and Redwing rode off, I waved goodbye, then Rascal and I shared my sandwich. How long was *soon* to Twilight? When we finished our lunch, Twilight still hadn't arrived, so I lounged in a patch of sunshine for a while, while Rascal napped. Finally, we started walking home, me throwing sticks and Rascal chasing them. He still hadn't learned the fetching part but it didn't matter. There were tons of sticks to throw.

Twilight found us about twenty minutes later. She let me put the halter on her head, then jump aboard, this time without a mounting block. When she moved off, her stride felt elastic and strong. She was already getting used to carrying a rider.

We practiced the reins for a while since if I ever had to shut down my horse-sense, we both still wanted to communicate with each other. I was amazed at how good she was at it all. Stop, right, left, leg cues, slower, faster. Twilight caught onto everything so quickly it was like she was born to be a saddle horse. Of course, it helped to be able to explain everything to her too.

Then she asked me to take her halter off.

*Why?*

*Surprise.*

Okay, so this was weird. What could Twilight surprise me with that needed me to take her halter off? I wanted to know, more than anything.

When it was off her head, she told me to tie Rascal to a tree.

*Back soon?* I asked, worried about him.

*Soon.*

Hopefully this *soon* was a little shorter than the last one. Still, anticipation filled me as I jumped onto her bare back. I put out my hand toward Rascal. "Stay," I said.

He whined, cocked his head, and sat down.

"Stay," I repeated. He lay down and flopped his head on his paws, obviously resigned to waiting for our return.

When Twilight sprang into a lope, I only had one twinge of nervousness. I hadn't spent much time in this part of the country and had no idea where we were going – but then I remembered that Twilight knew this country like she knew the bottom of her grain bucket. No way were we getting lost.

We loped through the trees and along deer trails for ten minutes, then reached the edge of the forest. Twilight stopped.

*Ready?*

*Ready for what?*

*Fun!* And she sprang forward. In one second, she was racing full out, her head high and her legs stretching and pulling back like pistons in a powerful engine, carrying us over the ground faster than I'd ever gone in my life. We covered that meadow in a matter of seconds, galloped through a tiny forest, and broke into a second, larger meadow.

I saw them in an instant. Every head turned toward us, small and big, dark and light, blaze, starred, and unmarked. Twilight's herd, with one addition, a pretty little sorrel with a wide blaze and four white legs. Some mix ups had been bound to happen with all the herds mashed together in the corrals and I was glad Twilight's herd had benefited from that. Their family had had far too many losses lately.

Night Hawk trotted toward us and sounded a warning. I ducked over Twilight's neck, so they wouldn't see me.

She neighed to her sire and he returned her call, sounding much friendlier. Twilight angled toward the herd in such a way that they wouldn't see me as clearly, and when she reached them, didn't stop to greet her sire or the lead mare, didn't go sniff noses with Wind Dancer or Butterfly, knowing they would discover me. Instead, she kept running in a big circle around them.

And the next thing I knew, Ice was galloping along behind us. Then Butterfly was stretching her impossibly long legs beside us, trying to match her big sister stride for stride. Not to be left behind, Wind Dancer neighed loudly, then raced up to run on Twilight's other side, her long, tangled mane whipping back like foam off a wave, her thick, creamy tail streaming behind her.

The white faced sorrel came alongside Butterfly – and she had sky blue eyes! I touched her mind. Shimmer! Her name was Shimmer. How fantastic! I looked back over my shoulder. Night Hawk and Black Wing were running behind too, their heads as high as their spirits.

I wanted to sit up straight on Twilight's back, my arms wide as I embraced the thunder of their hooves, the scent of their bodies, the heat of the sun on my head, and the wind lashing my skin – but I knew it would only scare them and ruin everything, so I only did it in my mind. I was racing with the wild horses! I was one of them! For the first time in my life, instead of just feeling what they felt as they ran, joyous and carefree, I was actually in the middle of the herd, running, leaping, playing...

It was the perfect gift. The perfect surprise. Life could not get any better than this moment. *Ever*.

Later, as we quietly rode back to get Rascal, I couldn't talk, not even mind-talk. I had run with the mustangs, and it had been the most magical experience of my life.

Rascal was waiting impatiently but quietly for us. He danced around after I untied him, waiting for me to remove the rope from the tree, then rushed around me in circles as I walked back to Twilight.

*Thank you!*

Twilight's pleasure warmed my heart. She was happy I liked her gift so much.

*Extra oats tonight?* I asked her.

*Yes!*

Well, that certainly got a response. I smiled as I moved around to her side, the halter hanging on my arm.

*Halter?* she asked, slightly puzzled.

*Not now.* I smiled. Though I would have to use it at times in the future, out here in our real home, it simply wasn't necessary.

I jumped onto her back and we started off through the trees toward home, the halter and rope lying coiled across her golden shoulders. I played with her long, dark mane as we walked along, Rascal scooting energetically around us, capturing every scent he could find inside his curious nose.

It had been the most amazing day. Here I'd thought yesterday was going to be my lucky day, and honestly, it hadn't been bad: winning a race, rescuing mustangs. It couldn't have gotten much better, but still, it didn't compare with today.

Today had been my truly lucky day: my first ride on Twilight, the candid talk with Mom, her getting back to her painting, and then running with the mustangs. What more could I say than "Wow"?

And there was one thing more, maybe the most important thing of all. I now knew, with a certainty I couldn't describe with any words, that I could trust Twilight. Without exception, she would be there for me, through anything, through everything. I could trust her with my hopes and dreams, and I could trust her to always care for me, just as I would always care for her.

I could trust her with my life.

I smiled to myself as we wove through the trees. Knowing the way adventure seemed to always find us, it was only a matter of time until my life *was* in her very capable hooves. And that was okay.

But since this was my lucky day, maybe it wouldn't be today.

**What will happen next?**

Please turn the page

for a sneak preview

of the next book

# Whinnies on the Wind
### Volume 8

# **Autumn of Angels**

Available at:

**www.ponybooks.com**

# Chapter 1

I didn't realize that Rusty, my fantastic gray gelding, was feeling down until the day Kestrel and I decided to ride the horses to the hot mud pool. I'd been looking forward to our excursion for days. We were going to have a picnic on the edge of the hidden hot pool, situated way back in the deep dark woods, then wade around in our swim suits. Hang out. Talk. All that good stuff.

Since the pool was so far away, we needed to leave early. Right after breakfast, I tucked my lunch into my small backpack, said goodbye to Mom, and headed out the door. Twilight, my three-year-old mustang filly, met me halfway to the barn and eagerly followed me inside the big building to see Rusty leaning impatiently over his stall door.

"Hey, Rusty." My buddy pressed his gray head against my body and breathed deep as I rubbed him behind his ears. "You ready to go?" Of course, he didn't understand me. I was talking English, not doing the mind speaking.

Oh yeah. I haven't told you about that yet. Yes, I can mind-talk to my horses. I know, it's weird. Rusty and I were the ones who developed the rudimentary thought language years ago, but I can talk to Twilight and a couple of other horses too.

Most, however, don't really like language. Imagine an alien voice suddenly sounding in your head, and you'll understand why. I can still communicate with other horses though – so long as they're within my range of a mile – just not with words. I sense their emotions and can even send emotions to them, like calmness to a frightened horse, or happiness to one I'm glad to see.

I can even feel the physical sensations that horses experience. Believe me, there's nothing like the splash of cold water on your stomach as a nearby horse cools herself in the lake – I say "herself" because usually that horse is Twilight, trying to shock me. She's a brat. What more can I say?

Also, just so you know, I didn't ask for this gift. It's just the way I was born. I didn't do anything to deserve it, but most of the time I'm grateful for it. At least I had someone to talk to as I grew up in the wilderness other than my reclusive mother and my best friend – my *only* friend – Kestrel, who I usually see only once a week. Rusty, who has been with me since I was three, literally can be thanked as the one who made me normal, or as normal as I'm going to get.

I kissed his long nose, then walked toward the feed/tack room to get his saddle and bridle. I didn't get far. The door was blocked by Twilight. The big buckskin filly stamped her hoof and looked irritated.

Determined not to let any grumps ruin my day, I edged around her and reached to turn the doorknob.

She pressed against the door, stopping me.

I stepped back. *What wrong?* I asked, putting my hands on my hips.

*My turn.*

Ah. Yes. It was her turn. But she knew I only rode her on the days when we weren't going too far. She was only three-years-old and I didn't want to stress her legs before she'd matured. Bushwhacking can be super strenuous, especially when you're packing a human around.

*Long way*, I said.

*My turn. Will go slow.*

Wow, she really wanted me to ride her if she was promising to go slow. *Okay*. I stroked her neck, then straightened some of her heavy dark mane. *Your turn*.

I was kind of glad in a way. I love riding Twilight. I love riding Rusty too, but he's so steady and calm, whereas Twilight is pretty exciting. And besides, I'd ridden Rusty yesterday.

Twilight moved away from the feed/tack room door so I could grab her halter and some brushes, and a few minutes later, she was ready to go. Then a quick grooming for Rusty too, as he stood sedately in his stall with his head down, no longer remotely eager. That should have been my first clue, but all I was thinking about was the day ahead.

I first noticed something was wrong with Rusty right after we left, when he started lagging behind. Then, when we met up with Kestrel, riding her elderly bay mare, Twitchy, he dropped even farther back.

"What's wrong with Rusty?" Kestrel asked, shortly after we turned off the last trail. We couldn't even see him, the bush was so thick.

"I don't know. I asked him, but he's ignoring me."

"Maybe he's just relaxing."

I nodded. "Let's wait for him, okay?"

With all the lagging and waiting it took twice as long to get to the pool, but we finally made it – though when we first rode into the clearing, I wasn't sure we had arrived. Surely, the hot pool had been bigger than this when we saw it last spring. It looked inviting then. Now it just seemed like a hole of murky water.

"*This* is why we've ridden all this way?" asked Kestrel, staring down from Twitchy's back with disdain.

"I thought it was bigger."

"And more water than slime and moss?"

I shrugged. "Let's check it out."

Kestrel and I slid from our horses' backs. She tied Twitchy to a nearby tree and I turned Twilight loose, then we stripped down to the swim suits we wore beneath our clothes.

The mucky wet hole didn't look any bigger from the ground. I touched the edge with my foot. A mud bubble burst. Warm mud oozed between my toes – and it felt surprisingly *wonderful*.

"Ooh."

"Ooh, as in gross or ooh, as in good."

"Good. Definitely good."

Kestrel looked at me like I was a little crazy, but I'm pretty good at ignoring her you're-totally-insane expression. I should be; I've seen it enough.

I reached down, down, down with my foot – and when the mud reached mid-calf, I touched solid ground. Slowly, I transferred my weight to the mud-pool foot.

"Seriously? It's nice?"

"It's awesome." I stepped completely inside the pool, then sat on the mossy bank. My lower legs felt like they were in leg heaven. Kestrel sat across from me and touched one big toe to the mud. When nothing bad happened to it, she lowered her foot inch by inch into the mucky water.

*Call when going*, said Twilight.

*Okay.* I looked around for Rusty. He was nowhere in sight.

*Rusty?*

No answer. I sent out my horse radar. He was nearby.

"So talking to the horses again instead of me?" Both of her legs were in the mud now.

I smiled sheepishly. "Sorry. I was just wondering where Rusty is."

She flipped a foot at me and a mud blob hit my swim suit. "He's right over there." She pointed with her big toe.

And sure enough, there he was, back in the trees, his cute gray face barely visible between distant tree trunks. And he was watching us.

*Rusty, come see the pool.*

His face disappeared as he turned away from me. What?

*Are you sick?*

*Eat*, he replied.

But he couldn't be hungry. He'd eaten a full breakfast not too long ago, plus had probably snacked all the way to the pool. What else could've he been doing as he lagged behind?

*Rusty, are you okay?* Maybe he'd answer me this time.

*Fine.*

"What's wrong with him?" asked Kestrel.

"He's hungry."

"Sounds like Twitchy. She's always hungry." Kestrel flipped more mud on me. "Hey, this *is* fun."

"So glad you're enjoying yourself." I looked again for Rusty but he was gone. There was more going on with him than simple hunger, I could feel it.

Kestrel noticed my worry. "He's probably just enjoying his freedom now that you're riding Twilight. He's been packing you around for years."

"Yeah, you're right," I replied, though the thought didn't make me feel much better. I hoped Rusty didn't see me as a burden.

The rest of the morning was great. Mucky pools might be filthy and slimy and even a little stinky, but they're delightful too. The only down side was that there was something about being in a muddy pool that made

Kestrel want to coat me with mud. And of course, I couldn't just let her do it without getting her back.

Finally, when we looked more like lumpy chocolate statues than fourteen-year-old girls, she stopped torturing me and we sat at the edge of the pool again, grins bright in our muddy faces.

"You look hilarious."

"Not as funny as you." I expected a snappy comeback but instead, Kestrel's gaze shifted to the trees on the other side of the pool. She sighed and her smile slid from her face. She looked a million miles away.

"What's wrong?" Everyone was being weird today.

"What do you mean?"

"I don't know. You seem all serious all of a sudden."

Kestrel looked down at her muddy hands. "I have something to tell you and you're not going to like it."

My whole body stiffened. "What?"

She looked at me, her eyes pleading. Uh oh, this was bad. "You remember last summer, when I almost went away to school, then changed my mind?"

My stomach plummeted to my knees. "You're going away to boarding school."

Kestrel nodded. "I'm really sorry." She gave me a moment to respond and when I didn't, kept talking. "I'm going to miss this place so much though. Well, not the pool, but everything else. Our ranch. Mom and Dad. The horses. Riding. You." Her eyes met mine. "Okay, so maybe the pool too," she added and smiled weakly. "Just a little."

"So why go then?"

"I just… it's not that there's anything wrong here. There's just so much out there, in the world. I want to start seeing it. And it's more than that too. It makes sense for me. It's a great school and Mom and Dad can afford it right now. Maybe next year they won't be able to, and I want to have at least one year that I'm not home schooled before I head off to University." She paused for a long moment, then cleared her throat and continued. "And I was wondering, hoping, you'd want to try again. You know, asking your mom if you can come with me. She's painting again. She might have enough money, and I'm sure you can get in. You're totally smart, in a weird, unique kind of way."

I almost laughed, despite the fact that my world was collapsing around me. Only Kestrel would think that was a compliment. What was I going to do without her for months on end? With just Mom, Rusty, and Twilight to talk to? How lonely life would be with Kestrel gone.

And if I went, I'd have my best friend, plus a whole bunch of other girls to hang out with. I'd make more friends. I'd experience a completely different sort of life, life in the city. Scary, but exciting and different too.

And bonus, I could investigate the mystery that had surrounded my life! I'd found a few clues over the years, though none of them had come willingly from Mom. In fact, I'd quit asking her about her past because it was a waste of time. But if I went away to school, I'd have access to computers and telephones and all those modern conveniences, and I could find the truth.

I know it's not normal for kids to think about a parent's past this way, but you have to understand, my mom's secrets aren't little ones. First, she's a hermit living under a fake name, and we're hiding out in the bush, or rather she's hiding *me*, as I eventually discovered, from either her family or my dad's family. I saw some of these mysterious relatives last spring, though they didn't see me: a girl who had to be my cousin because she looked so much like me, and her grandmother. If she was my cousin, maybe *my* grandmother. Scary thought. If you'd ever seen this grandmother, you'd agree.

And Mom's mystery has something to do with someone named Tristan too. Last spring I snuck a peek at some papers she'd gotten from a private investigator, and saw a birth certificate for someone name Tristan. I didn't have time to read the last name.

"Evy?"

"Uh, sorry," I said, my mind racing to remember what we'd been talking about. Oh yeah, asking Mom if I could go to school. "Do you really think she'd let me?"

"Maybe." Pause. "Well, honestly? I doubt it." I could always count on Kestrel to tell me what she was really thinking, even when it was the last thing I wanted to hear and the last thing she wanted to say. "But it won't hurt to try," she added brightly. "If you don't ask, it's an automatic *no*."

"True."

"And we'd have so much fun – you have no idea how much! We could even investigate your mom's past."

I nodded. "I thought of that too."

"But you'd have to leave Rusty and Twilight behind."

"Yeah, that would suck." But maybe it wouldn't be as bad as what I thought. Maybe Kestrel was right and Rusty was tired of having to haul me all over the place. I knew if I could be one thing, it was a pain in the neck, and he'd been taking care of me for eleven years. He deserved a break. Twilight too, might not mind if I left for a few months. She could spend the school year with her herd, hanging out and being a wild horse again for a while. I knew she found domestic life a bit stifling and she only stayed because of me and Rusty. With me gone, she could have a long visit with her family, and hey, maybe even take Rusty with her. That might be nice for him, as long as Night Hawk, the herd leader and Twilight's sire allowed him to spend the winter with them.

"Sooo? Talking to the horses again? You have to stop doing that, especially if we go to school. It looks weird. You get all spacey and zoned out."

"Sorry. I was just thinking about going."

"Really? Awesome!" She flicked more mud on me. "We could go to concerts and malls and join sports teams and…" And Kestrel was off and running. I have to admit that it was kind of fun to brainstorm all the things we could do in the city. It wasn't until we got down to climbing Grouse Mountain every day and entering skateboarding competitions that I started to wonder if it might be too much work to go. But it was too late. There was no stopping Kestrel now.

On the way home, we continued to dream out loud, thinking up things I might find when I solved my mom's hermit mystery, my favourite being that someone was looking for us because I was the secret heir to the kingdom of a small country.

Okay, not a small country. A big one.

Though we chipped away the drying mud as we rode back to my house, we were still pretty dirty by the time we arrived, so we rode the horses behind the house to the little lake and dismounted to wash. The cool water felt lovely after all that heat, and the mud seemed to melt away.

Kestrel still wasn't slowing down. Now she was figuring out what we should say to Mom to convince her to let me go. "Maybe you can tell her that you want to be a Geomatics major in University and—"

"A what?" I asked. "A geo… matrix…"

"Geomatics. I have no idea what they do, but apparently it's a hard degree to get. You're going to need more specialized courses if you're going to be accepted into that program."

"But Mom has to believe me too." I laughed. "And she isn't going to believe I want to learn Geomatics when I can't even tell her what it is."

"What *will* she believe?"

"That I want to work with horses, but I don't know if you can do that in University. I might have to go to one of those specialty schools or something."

"A vet. That's what you should say."

It was true that a vet would need to go to University, but I didn't really want to be a vet. And besides, Rusty hated it when I lied, *really* hated it. If I even thought about lying, he got totally upset.

I looked around. Where *was* Rusty?

Twitchy and Twilight stood on the shore, both grazing, but Rusty wasn't with them. He'd trailed behind us at a distance as we'd ridden home, but surely he would've arrived by now. I cast out my radar. He was in the barn.

In the barn. Already?

He really *was* sick!

"Something's wrong with Rusty," I said, suddenly feeling breathless. If anything bad happened to him, I'd never... I couldn't... well, it would be beyond horrible in every way I could possibly think of.

Kestrel was right beside me as we ran around the tiny cabin and raced toward the barn. Halfway there, Twilight galloped past us, her ebony tail flowing behind her like a flag. Her dust cloud enveloped us, clinging to our wet legs. A dirt clod flew past my ear.

"Twilight!"

She ran into the barn, completely ignoring us.

"Does she know what's wrong with Rusty?" Kestrel gasped beside me.

"No. She's thinking about oats."

We burst into the barn to see Twilight at the feed/tack room door, looking all eager, and Rusty standing at his stall, looking more dejected than I've ever seen him in my life. The poor guy! He looked like he was about to drop any second.

I rushed to his side and reached to feel the tips of his ears. If they were too hot or cold... but Rusty raised his head so I couldn't touch them. Weird. I knew he didn't like to admit any weakness but I needed to check him out if he wasn't feeling well. Maybe I could check his breathing. I put my hand in front of his nose to feel his exhalations – and Rusty pushed my hand away, gently to be sure, but still a push.

"What's wrong with him?" asked Kestrel.

"I don't know."

I heard Twilight leave the feed/tack room door and walk toward us, probably thinking to hurry the oat-getting a little, and suddenly Rusty was all action and temper. Kestrel squeaked and we both stumbled back as he jumped toward Twilight, teeth bared and not looking at all like the Rusty I'd known and loved my entire life.

Twilight easily avoided him – growing up in the wild had made her quick – and trotted toward the door. *Call me for oats*, she said as she left the barn.

Rusty deflated again the moment she was gone.

What on earth was wrong with him? He had to be feeling terrible. Where did he hurt? What should I do?

*Not sick*, he said, and hung his head.

Not taking his word for it, I zoned into what he was feeling. And he was right, he wasn't feeling sick – or at least there was no physical pain or discomfort. What

Rusty felt was sadness, or to be more accurate, an intense wretchedness and desolation. It fell over me like a suffocating blanket, thick and unwieldy.

I didn't get it. What had happened to make him feel this way? It was as if his best friend had died or something, and in his pain, he'd lashed out at Twilight. I was just glad that she was a practical horse and wouldn't hold a grudge. She'd just think Rusty was having a bad day.

But this was a lot more than a bad day; I'd known Rusty almost all my life and I'd never felt this from him before. I had no clue what was wrong, or what to do. But his desolation was real, totally and completely real – and it was *my* job to stick by him and cheer him up. I had to help him, just as he'd helped me countless times in countless ways in the past.

If I could just figure out what to do.

CPSIA information can be obtained
at www.ICGtesting.com
Printed in the USA
LVHW020326211021
701032LV00019B/484

9 781927 100288